"“Oh, good God,” he kept saying with great relish. “Good God . . .”"

ANTON CHEKHOV

Gooseberries

Translated by
Ronald Wilks

Contents

The Kiss

On 20 May, at eight o'clock in the evening, all six batteries of a reserve artillery brigade, on their way back to headquarters, stopped for the night at the village of Mestechki. At the height of all the confusion – some officers were busy with the guns, while others had assembled in the main square by the churchyard fence to receive their billetings – someone in civilian dress rode up from behind the church on a strange horse: it was small and dun-coloured with a fine neck and short tail, and seemed to move sideways instead of straight ahead, making small dancing movements with its legs as if they were being whipped. When the rider came up to the officers he doffed his hat and said, 'Our squire, His Excellency, Lieutenant-General von Rabbeck, invites you for tea and would like you to come now . . .'

The horse performed a bow and a little dance, and retreated with the same sideways motion. The rider raised his hat again and quickly disappeared behind the church on his peculiar horse.

'To hell with it!' some of the officers grumbled as they rode off to their quarters. 'We want to sleep and up pops this von Rabbeck with his tea! We know what *that* means all right!'

Every officer in the six batteries vividly remembered the previous year when they were on manoeuvres with officers from a Cossack regiment and had received a similar invitation from a landowning count, who was a retired officer. This hospitable and genial count had plied them with food and drink, would not hear of them returning to their billets and made them stay the night. That was all very well, of course, and they could not have hoped for better. But the trouble was that this retired officer was overjoyed beyond measure at having young men as his guests and he regaled them with stories from his glorious past until dawn, led them on a tour of the house, showed them his valuable paintings, old engravings and rare guns, and read out signed letters from eminent personages; and all this time the tired and weary officers listened, looked, pined for bed, and continuously yawned in their sleeves. When their host finally let them go, it was too late for bed.

Now, was this von Rabbeck one of the same breed? Whether he was or not, there was nothing they could do about it. The officers put clean uniforms on, smartened themselves up and went off en masse to look for the squire's house. On the square by the church they were told that they could either take the lower path leading down to the river behind the church, and then go along the bank to the garden, or they could ride direct from the church along the higher road which would bring them to the count's barns about a quarter of a mile from the village. The officers decided on the higher route.

'Who is this von Rabbeck?' they argued as they rode along. 'Is he the one who commanded a cavalry division at Plevna?'

'No, that wasn't von Rabbeck, just Rabbe, and without the "von".'

'It's marvellous weather, anyway!'

The road divided when they reached the first barn: one fork led straight on and disappeared in the darkness of the evening, while the other turned towards the squire's house on the right. The officers took the right fork and began to lower their voices . . . Stone barns with red tiled roofs stood on both sides of the road and they had the heavy, forbidding look of some provincial barracks. Ahead of them were the lighted windows of the manor-house.

'That's a good sign, gentlemen!' one of the officers said. 'Our setter's going on in front. That means he scents game!'

Lieutenant Lobytko, a tall, strongly built officer, who was riding ahead of the others, who had no moustache (although he was over twenty-five there wasn't a trace of hair on his face), and who was renowned in the brigade for his keen senses and ability to sniff a woman out from miles away, turned round and said, 'Yes, there must be women here, my instinct tells me.'

The officers were met at the front door by von Rabbeck himself – a fine-looking man of about sixty, wearing civilian clothes. He said how very pleased and happy he was to see the officers as he shook hands, but begged them most sincerely, in the name of God, to excuse him for not inviting them to stay the night, as two sisters with their children, his brothers and some neighbours had turned up, and he didn't have one spare room.

The general shook everyone's hand, apologized and smiled, but they could tell from his face that he wasn't nearly as pleased to have guests as last year's count and he had only asked them as it was the done thing. And, as they climbed the softly carpeted stairs and listened, the officers sensed that they had been invited only because it would have caused embarrassment if they had *not* been invited. At the sight of footmen dashing around lighting the lamps in the hall and upstairs, they felt they had introduced a note of uneasiness and anxiety into the house. And how could any host be pleased at having nineteen strange officers descend on a house where two sisters, children, brothers and neighbours had already arrived, most probably to celebrate some family anniversary. They were met in the ballroom upstairs by a tall, stately old lady with black eyebrows and a long face – the living image of Empress Eugénie. She gave them a majestic, welcoming smile and said how glad and happy she was to have them as guests and apologized for the fact that she and her husband weren't able to invite the officers to stay overnight on this occasion. Her beautiful, majestic smile, which momentarily disappeared every time she turned away from her guests, revealed that in her day she had seen many officers, that she had no time for them now, and that she had invited them and was apologizing only because her upbringing and social position demanded it.

The officers entered the large dining-room where about ten gentlemen and ladies, old and young, were sitting along one side of the table having tea. Behind their chairs, enveloped in a thin haze of cigar smoke, was a group of men with a rather lean, young, red-whiskered man in the middle, rolling his 'r's as he spoke out loud in English. Behind them, through a door, was a bright room with light blue furniture.

'Gentlemen, there's so many of you, it's impossible to

introduce *everyone*!' the general was saying in a loud voice, trying to sound cheerful. 'So don't stand on ceremony, introduce yourselves!'

Some officers wore very serious, even solemn expressions; others forced a smile, and all of them felt awkward as they bowed rather indifferently and sat down to tea.

Staff-Captain Ryabovich, a short, stooping officer, with spectacles and lynx-like side whiskers, was more embarrassed than anyone else. While his fellow-officers were trying to look serious or force a smile, his face, lynx-like whiskers and spectacles seemed to be saying, 'I'm the shyest, most modest and most insignificant officer in the whole brigade!' When he first entered the dining-room and sat down to tea, he found it impossible to concentrate on any one face or object. All those faces, dresses, cut-glass decanters, steaming glasses, moulded cornices, merged into one composite sensation, making Ryabovich feel ill at ease, and he longed to bury his head somewhere. Like a lecturer at his first appearance in public, he could see everything in front of him well enough, but at the same time he could make little sense of it (physicians call this condition, when someone sees without understanding, 'psychic blindness'). But after a little while Ryabovich began to feel more at home, recovered his normal vision and began to take stock of his surroundings. Since he was a timid and unsociable person, he was struck above all by what he himself had never possessed – the extraordinary boldness of these unfamiliar people. Von Rabbeck, two elderly ladies, a young girl in a lilac dress, and the young man with red whiskers – Rabbeck's youngest son – had sat themselves very cunningly among the officers, as though it had all been rehearsed. Straight away they had launched into a heated argument, which the guests could not help joining. The girl in lilac very excitedly insisted that the artillery had a much easier time than either the cavalry or the infantry, while Rabbeck and the elderly ladies argued the contrary. A rapid conversational crossfire ensued. Ryabovich glanced at the lilac girl who was arguing so passionately about something that was so foreign to her, so utterly boring, and he could see artificial smiles flickering over her face.

Von Rabbeck and family skilfully drew the officers into the argument, at the same time watching their wine glasses with eagle eyes to check whether they were filled, that they had enough sugar, and one officer who wasn't eating biscuits or drinking any brandy worried them. The more Ryabovich looked and listened, the more he began to like this insincere but wonderfully disciplined family.

After tea the officers went into the ballroom. Lieutenant Lobytko's instinct had not failed him: the room was full of girls and young married women. Already this 'setter' lieutenant had positioned himself next to a young blonde in a black dress, bending over dashingly as though leaning on some invisible sabre, smiling and flirting with his shoulders. Most probably he was telling her some intriguing nonsense as the blonde glanced superciliously at his well-fed face and said, 'Really?'

If that 'setter' had had any brains, that cool 'Really?' should have told him that he would never be called 'to heel'.

The grand piano suddenly thundered out. The sounds of a sad waltz drifted through the wide-open windows and everyone remembered that outside it was spring, an evening in May, and they smelt the fragrance of the young leaves of the poplars, of roses and lilac. Ryabovich, feeling the effects of the brandy and the music, squinted at a window, smiled and watched the movements of the women. Now it seemed that the fragrance of the roses, the poplars and lilac wasn't coming from the garden but from the ladies' faces and dresses.

Rabbeck's son had invited a skinny girl to dance and waltzed twice round the room with her. Lobytko glided over the parquet floor as he flew up to the girl in lilac and whirled her round the room. They all began to dance . . . Ryabovich stood by the door with guests who were not dancing and watched. Not once in his life had he danced, not once had he put his arm round an attractive young woman's waist. He would usually be absolutely delighted when, with everyone looking on, a man took a young girl he hadn't met before by the waist and offered his shoulders for her to rest her hands on, but he could never imagine himself in that situation. There had been times when he envied his fellow-officers' daring and dashing ways and it made him very depressed. The realization that he was shy, round-shouldered, quite undistinguished, that he had a long waist, lynx-like side whiskers, hurt him deeply. But over the years this realization had become something of a habit and as he watched his friends dance or talk out loud he no longer envied them but was filled with sadness.

When the quadrille began, young von Rabbeck went over to the officers who were not dancing and invited two of them to a game of billiards. They accepted and left the great hall with him. As he had nothing else to do, and feeling he would like to take at least some part in what was going on, Ryabovich trudged off after them. First they went into the drawing-room, then down a narrow corridor with a glass ceiling, then into a room where three sleepy footmen leapt up from a sofa the moment they entered. Finally, after passing through a whole series of rooms, young Rabbeck and company reached a small billiard-room and the game began.

Ryabovich, who never played any games except cards, stood by the table and indifferently watched the players, cue in hand, walking up and down in their unbuttoned tunics, making puns and shouting things he could not understand. The players ignored him, only turning round to say, 'I beg your pardon', when one of them happened accidentally to nudge him with an elbow or prod him with a cue. Even before the first game was over, he was bored and began to feel he was not wanted, that he was in the way . . . He felt drawn back to the ballroom and walked away.

As he walked back he had a little adventure. Halfway, he realized he was lost – he knew very well he had to go by those three sleepy footmen, but already he had passed through five or six rooms and those footmen seemed to have vanished into thin air. He realized his mistake, retraced his steps a little and turned to the right, only to find himself in a small, dimly lit room he had not seen on the way to the billiard-room. He stood still for a minute or so, opened the first door he came to with determination and entered a completely dark room. Ahead of him he could see light coming through a crack in the door and beyond was the muffled sound of a sad mazurka. The windows here had been left open as they had in the ballroom and he could smell poplars, lilac and roses . . .

Ryabovich stopped, undecided what to do . . . Just then he was astonished to hear hurried footsteps, the rustle of a dress and a female voice whispering breathlessly, 'At last!' Two soft, sweet-smelling arms (undoubtedly a woman's) encircled his neck, a burning cheek pressed against his and at the same time there was the sound of a kiss. But immediately after the kiss the woman gave a faint cry and shrank backwards in disgust – that was how it seemed to Ryabovich.

He was on the point of crying out too and he rushed towards the bright chink in the door.

His heart pounded away when he was back in the hall and his hands trembled so obviously that he hastily hid them behind his back. At first he was tormented by shame and he feared everyone there knew he had just been embraced and kissed, and this made him hesitate and look around anxiously. But when he had convinced himself that everyone was dancing and gossiping just as peacefully as before, he gave himself up to a totally new kind of sensation, one he had never experienced before in all his life. Something strange was happening to him . . . his neck, which just a few moments ago had been embraced by sweet-smelling hands, seemed anointed with oil. And on his left cheek, just by his moustache, there was a faint, pleasant, cold, tingling sensation, the kind you get from peppermint drops and the more he rubbed the spot the stronger the tingling became. From head to heels he was overcome by a strange, new feeling which grew stronger every minute. He wanted to dance, speak to everyone, run out into the garden, laugh out loud. He completely forgot his stoop, his insignificant appearance, his lynx-like whiskers and 'vague appearance' (once he happened to hear some ladies saying this about him). When Rabbeck's wife went by he gave her such a broad, warm smile that she stopped and gave him a very searching look.

'I love this house so much!' he said, adjusting his spectacles.

The general's wife smiled and told him that the house still belonged to her father. Then she asked if his parents were still alive, how long he had been in the army, why he was so thin, and so on . . . When Ryabovich had replied, she moved on, leaving him smiling even more warmly and he began to think he was surrounded by the most wonderful people . . .

Mechanically, Ryabovich ate and drank everything he was offered at the dinner table, deaf to everything as he tried to find an explanation for what had just happened. It was a mysterious, romantic incident, but it wasn't difficult to explain. No doubt some girl or young married woman had a rendezvous with someone in that dark room, had waited for a long time, and then mistook Ryabovich for her hero in her nervous excitement. This was the most likely explanation, all the more so as Ryabovich had hesitated in the middle of the room, which made it look as though he were expecting someone . . .

'But who *is* she?' he thought as he surveyed the ladies' faces. 'She must be young, as old ladies don't have rendezvous. And intelligent – I could tell from the rustle of her dress, her smell, her voice.'

He stared at the girl in lilac and found her very attractive.

She had beautiful shoulders and arms, a clever face and a fine voice. As he gazed at her, Ryabovich wanted *her*, no one else, to be that mysterious stranger . . . But she gave a rather artificial laugh and wrinkled her long nose, which made her look old. Then he turned to the blonde in black. She was younger, simpler and less affected, with charming temples and she sipped daintily from her wine glass. Now Ryabovich wanted her to be the stranger. But he soon discovered that she had a featureless face and he turned to her neighbour . . . 'It's hard to say,' he wondered dreamily. 'If I could just take the lilac girl's shoulders and arms away, add the blonde's temples, then take those eyes away from the girl on Lobytko's left, *then*.' He merged them all into one, so that he had an image of the girl who had kissed him, the image he desired so much, but which he just could not find among the guests around the table.

After dinner the officers, well-fed and slightly tipsy by now, began to make their farewells and expressed their thanks. Once again the hosts apologized for not having them stay the night.

'Delighted, gentlemen, absolutely delighted,' the general was saying and this time he meant it – probably because people are usually more sincere and better-humoured saying goodbye to guests than welcoming them.

'Delighted! Glad to see you back any time, so don't stand on ceremony. Which way are you going? The higher road? No, go through the garden, it's quicker.'

The officers went into the garden, where it seemed very dark and quiet after the bright lights and the noise. They did not say a word all the way to the gate. They were half-drunk, cheerful and contented, but the darkness and the silence made them pause for thought. Probably they were thinking the same as Ryabovich: would they ever see the day when they would own a large house, have a family, a garden, when *they* too would be able to entertain people (however much of a pretence this might be), feed them well, make them drunk and happy?

As they went through the garden gate they all started talking at once and, for no apparent reason, laughed out loud. Now they were descending the path that led down to the river and then ran along the water's edge, weaving its way around the bushes, the little pools of water and the willows which overhung the river. The bank and the path were barely visible, and the far side was plunged in darkness. Here and there were reflections of the stars in the water, quivering and breaking up into little patches – the only sign that the river was flowing fast. All was quiet. Sleepy sandpipers called plaintively from the far bank and on the near side a nightingale in a bush poured out its song, ignoring the passing officers.

The men paused by the bush, touched it, but still the nightingale sang.

'That's a bird for you!' approving voices murmured. 'Here we are, right next to him and he doesn't take a blind bit of notice! What a rascal!'

The path finally turned upwards and came out on to the high road by the church fence. The officers were exhausted from walking up the hill and sat down for a smoke. On the far bank they could make out a dim red light and they tried to pass the time by guessing whether it was a camp fire, a light in a window, or something else . . . Ryabovich looked at it and imagined that the light was winking at him and smiling, as though it knew all about that kiss.

When he reached his quarters Ryabovich quickly undressed and lay on his bed. In the same hut were Lobytko and Lieutenant Merzlyakov, a gentle, rather quiet young man, who was considered well-educated in his own little circle. He was always reading the *European Herald* when he had the chance and took it with him everywhere. Lobytko undressed, paced up and down for a long time, with the expression of a dissatisfied man, and sent the batman for some beer.

Merzlyakov lay down, placed a candle near his pillow and immersed himself in the *European Herald*.

'Who *is* she?' Ryabovich wondered as he glanced at the grimy ceiling. His neck still felt as if it had been anointed with oil and he had that tingling sensation around his mouth – just like peppermint drops. He had fleeting visions of the lilac girl's shoulders and arms, the temples and truthful eyes of the blonde in black, waists, dresses, brooches. He tried to fix these visions firmly in his mind, but they kept dancing about, dissolving, flickering. When these visions vanished completely against that darkened background everyone has when he closes his eyes, he began to hear hurried steps, rustling dresses, the sound of a kiss and he was gripped by an inexplicable, overwhelming feeling of joy. Just as he was abandoning himself to it, he heard the batman come back and report that there wasn't any beer. Lobytko became terribly agitated and started pacing up and down again.

'Didn't I tell you he's an idiot?' he said, stopping first in front of Ryabovich, then Merzlyakov. 'A man must really be a blockhead and idiot to come back without any beer! The man's a rogue, eh?'

'Of course, you won't find any beer in this place,' Merzlyakov said without taking his eyes off the *European Herald.*

'Oh, do you really think so?' Lobytko persisted. 'Good God, put me on the moon and I'll find you beer and women right away! Yes, I'll go now and find some . . . Call me a scoundrel if I don't succeed!'

He slowly dressed and pulled on his high boots. Then he finished his cigarette in silence and left.

'Rabbeck, Grabbeck, Labbeck,' he muttered, pausing in the hall. 'I don't feel like going on my own, dammit! Fancy a little walk, Ryabovich?'

There was no reply, so he came back, slowly undressed and got into bed. Merzlyakov sighed, put the *European Herald* away and snuffed the candle.

'Hm,' Lobytko murmured as he puffed his cigarette in the dark.

Ryabovich pulled the blankets over his head, curled himself into a ball and tried to merge the visions fleeting through his mind into one fixed image. But he failed completely. Soon he fell asleep and his last waking thought was of someone caressing him and making him happy, of something absurd and unusual, but nonetheless exceptionally fine and joyful, that had entered his life. And his dreams centred around this one thought.

When he woke up, the sensation of oil on his cheek and the minty tingling near his lips had vanished, but the joy of yesterday still filled his heart. Delighted, he watched the window frames, gilded now by the rising sun, and listened intently to the street noises. Outside, just by the window, he could hear loud voices – Lebedetsky, Ryabovich's battery commander, who had just caught up with the brigade, was shouting at his sergeant – simply because he had lost the habit of talking softly.

'Is there anything else?' he roared.

'When they were shoeing yesterday, sir, someone drove a nail into Pigeon's hoof. The medical orderly put clay and vinegar on it and they're keeping the horse reined, away from the others. And artificer Artemyev got drunk yesterday and the lieutenant had him tied to the fore-carriage of an auxiliary field-gun.'

And the sergeant had more to report. Karpov had forgotten the new cords for the trumpets and the stakes for the tents, and the officers had spent the previous evening as guests of General von Rabbeck. During the conversation, Lebedetsky's head and red beard appeared at the window. He blinked his short-sighted eyes at the sleepy officers and bade them good morning.

'Everything all right?' he asked.

'One of the shaft-horses damaged its withers – it was the new collar,' Lobytko answered, yawning.

The commander sighed, pondered for a moment and said in a loud voice, 'I'm still wondering whether to pay Aleksandra a visit, I really ought to go and see how she is. Well, goodbye for now, I'll catch you up by evening.'

A quarter of an hour later the brigade moved off. As it passed the general's barns, Ryabovich looked to the right where the house was. The blinds were drawn in all the windows. Clearly, everyone was still asleep. And the girl who had kissed Ryabovich the day before was sleeping too. He tried to imagine her as she slept and he had a clear and distinct picture of the wide-open windows, the little green branches peeping into her bedroom, the morning freshness, the smell of poplars, lilac and roses, her bed and the chair with that dress which had rustled the day before lying over it, tiny slippers, a watch on the table. But the actual features of that face, that sweet, dreamy smile, exactly what was most characteristic of her, slipped through his imagination like mercury through the fingers. When he had ridden about a quarter of a mile, he looked back. The yellow church, the house, the river and garden were flooded in sunlight and the river, with its bright green banks and its waters reflecting the light blue sky and glinting silver here and there, looked very beautiful. Ryabovich took a last look at Mestechki and he felt so sad, as if he were saying farewell to what was very near and dear to him.

But there were only long-familiar, boring scenes ahead of him. On both sides of the road there were fields of young rye and buckwheat, where crows were hopping about. Ahead, all he could see was dust and the backs of soldiers' heads; and behind, the same dust, the same faces. The brigade was led by a vanguard of four soldiers bearing sabres and behind them rode the military choristers, followed by trumpeters. Every now and then, like torchbearers in a funeral cortège, the vanguard and singers ignored the regulation distance and pushed on far ahead. Ryabovich rode alongside the first field-gun of the fifth battery and he could see the other four in front. These long, ponderous processions formed by brigades on the move can strike civilians as very peculiar, an unintelligible muddle, and non-military people just cannot fathom why a single field-gun has to be escorted by so many soldiers, why it has to be drawn by so many horses all tangled up in such strange harness, as if it really was such a terrible, heavy object. But Ryabovich understood everything perfectly well and for that reason he found it all extremely boring. He had long known why a hefty bombardier always rides with the officer at the head of every battery and why he is called an outrider. Immediately behind this bombardier came the riders on the first, then the middle-section trace-horses. Ryabovich knew that the horses to the left were saddle-horses, while those on the right were auxiliary – all this was very boring. The horsemen were followed by two shaft-horses, one ridden by a horseman with yesterday's dust still on his back and who had a clumsy-looking, very comical piece of wood fixed to his right leg. Ryabovich knew what it was for and did not find it funny. All the riders waved their whips mechanically and shouted now and again. As for the field-gun, it was an ugly thing. Sacks of oats covered with tarpaulin lay on the fore-carriage and the gun itself was hung with kettles, kit-bags and little sacks: it resembled a small harmless animal which had been surrounded, for some reason, by men and horses. On the side sheltered from the wind a team of six strode along, swinging their arms. This gun was followed by more bombardiers, riders, shaft-horses and another field-gun – just as ugly and uninspiring as the first – lumbering along in the rear. After the second gun came a third, then a fourth with an officer riding alongside (there are six batteries to a brigade and four guns to a battery). The whole procession stretched about a quarter of a mile and ended with the baggage wagons, where a most likeable creature plodded thoughtfully along, his long-eared head drooping: this was Magar the donkey, brought from Turkey by a certain battery commander.

Ryabovich looked apathetically at all those necks and faces in front and behind. At any other time he would have dozed off, but now he was immersed in new, pleasant thoughts. When the brigade had first set off, he had tried to convince himself that the incident of the kiss was only some unimportant, mysterious adventure and that essentially it was trivial and too ridiculous for serious thought. But very quickly he waved logic aside and gave himself up to his dreams. First he pictured himself in von Rabbeck's drawing-room, sitting next to a girl who resembled both the girl in lilac and the blonde in black. Then he closed his eyes and imagined himself with another, completely strange girl, with very indeterminate features: in his thoughts he spoke to her, caressed her and leaned his head on her shoulder. Then he thought of war and separation, reunion, dinner with his wife and children . . .

'Brakes on!' rang out the command every time they went downhill. He shouted the command too, and feared that his own shouts would shatter his daydreams and bring him back to reality.

As they passed some estate, Ryabovich peeped over the fence into the garden. There he saw a long avenue, straight as a ruler, strewn with yellow sand and lined with young birches. With the eagerness of a man who has surrendered himself to daydreaming, he imagined tiny female feet walking over the yellow sand. And, quite unexpectedly, he had a clear mental picture of the girl who had kissed him, the girl he had visualized the previous evening during dinner. This image had planted itself in his mind and would not leave him.

At midday someone shouted from a wagon in the rear, 'Attention, eyes left! Officers!'

The brigadier drove up in an open carriage drawn by two white horses. He ordered it to stop near the second battery and shouted something no one understood. Several officers galloped over to him, Ryabovich among them.

'Well, what's the news?' asked the brigadier, blinking his red eyes. 'Anyone ill?'

When they had replied, the brigadier, a small skinny man, chewed for a moment, pondered and then turned to one of the officers: 'One of your drivers, on the third gun, has taken his knee-guard off and the devil's hung it on the fore-carriage. Reprimand him!'

He looked up at Ryabovich and continued: 'It strikes me your harness breeches are too long.'

After a few more tiresome comments, the brigadier glanced at Lobytko and grinned. 'You look down in the dumps today, Lieutenant Lobytko. Pining for Madame Lopukhov, eh? Gentlemen, he's pining for Madame Lopukhov!'

Madame Lopukhov was a very plump, tall lady, well past forty. The brigadier, who had a passion for large women, no matter what age, suspected his officers nurtured similar passions. They smiled politely. Then the brigadier, delighted with himself for having made a very amusing, cutting remark, roared with laughter, tapped his driver on the back and saluted. The carriage drove off.

'All the things I'm dreaming about now and which seem impossible, out of this world, are in fact very ordinary,' Ryabovich thought as he watched the clouds of dust rising in the wake of the brigadier's carriage. 'It's all so very ordinary, everyone experiences it . . . The brigadier, for example. He was in love once, now he's married, with children. Captain Vachter is married and loved, despite having an extremely ugly red neck and no waistline. Salmanov is coarse and too much of a Tartar, but *he* had an affair that finished in marriage. I'm the same as everyone else . . . sooner or later I'll have to go through what they did . . .'

And he was delighted and encouraged by the thought that he was just an ordinary man, leading an ordinary life. Now he was bold enough to picture *her* and his happiness as much as he liked and he gave full rein to his imagination.

In the evening, when the brigade had reached its destination and the officers were resting in their tents, Ryabovich, Merzlyakov and Lobytko gathered round a trunk and had supper. Merzlyakov took his time, holding his *European Herald* on his knees and reading it as he slowly munched his food.

Lobytko could not stop talking and kept filling his glass with beer, while Ryabovich, whose head was rather hazy from dreaming all day long, said nothing as he drank. Three glasses made him tipsy and weak and he felt an irrepressible longing to share his new feelings with his friends.

'A strange thing happened to me at the Rabbecks,' he

said, trying to sound cool and sarcastic. 'I went to the billiard-room, you know . . .'

He began to tell them, in great detail, all about the kiss, but after a minute fell silent. In that one minute he had told them everything and he was astonished when he considered how little time was needed to tell his story: he had imagined it would take until morning. After he heard the story, Lobytko – who was a great liar and therefore a great sceptic – looked at him in disbelief and grinned. Merzlyakov twitched his eyebrows and kept his eyes glued to the *European Herald* as he calmly remarked, 'Damned if I know what to make of it! Throwing herself round a stranger's neck without saying a word first . . . She must have been a mental case . . .'

'Yes, some kind of neurotic,' Ryabovich agreed.

'Something similar happened to me once,' Lobytko said, assuming a frightened look. 'Last year I was travelling to Kovno . . . second class. The compartment was chock-full and it was impossible to sleep. So I tipped the guard fifty copeks . . . he took my luggage and got me a berth in a sleeper. I lay down and covered myself with a blanket. It was dark, you understand. Suddenly someone was touching my shoulder and breathing into my face. So I moved my arm and felt an elbow. I opened my eyes and – can you imagine! – it was a woman. Black eyes, lips as red as the best salmon, nostrils breathing passion, breasts like buffers! . . .'

'Just a minute,' Merzlyakov calmly interrupted. 'I don't dispute what you said about her breasts, but how could you see her lips if it was dark?'

Lobytko tried to wriggle out by poking fun at Merzlyakov's

obtuseness and this jarred on Ryabovich. He went away from the trunk, lay down and vowed never again to tell his secrets.

Camp life fell back into its normal routine. The days flashed by, each exactly the same as the other. All this time Ryabovich felt, thought and behaved like someone in love. When his batman brought him cold water in the mornings, he poured it over his head and each time he remembered that there was something beautiful and loving in his life.

In the evenings, when his fellow-officers talked about love and women, he would listen very attentively, sitting very close to them and assuming the habitual expression of a soldier hearing stories about battles he himself fought in. On those evenings when senior officers, led by 'setter' Lobytko, carried out 'sorties' on the local village, in true Don Juan style, Ryabovich went along with them and invariably returned feeling sad, deeply guilty and imploring *her* forgiveness. In his spare time, or on nights when he couldn't sleep, when he wanted to recall his childhood days, his parents, everything that was near and dear to him, he would always find himself thinking of Mestechki instead, of that strange horse, of von Rabbeck and his wife, who looked like the Empress Eugénie, of that dark room with the bright chink in the door.

On 31 August he left camp – not with his own brigade, however, but with two batteries. All the way he daydreamed and became very excited, as though he were going home. He wanted passionately to see that strange horse again, the church, those artificial Rabbecks, the dark room. Some inner voice, which so often deceives those in love, whispered that he was *bound* to see her again. And he was tormented by such questions as: how could he arrange a meeting, what would she say, had she forgotten the kiss? If the worst came to the worst, he would at least have the pleasure of walking through that dark room and remembering . . .

Towards evening, that familiar church and the white barns appeared on the horizon. His heart began to pound. He did not listen to what the officer riding next to him was saying, he was oblivious of everything and looked eagerly at the river gleaming in the distance, at the loft above which pigeons were circling in the light of the setting sun.

As he rode up to the church and heard the quartermaster speaking, he expected a messenger on horseback to appear from behind the fence any minute and invite the officers to tea . . . but the quartermaster read the billeting list out, the officers dismounted and strolled off into the village – and no messenger came.

'The people in the village will tell Rabbeck we're here and he'll send for us,' Ryabovich thought as he went into his hut. He just could not understand why a fellow-officer was lighting a candle, why the batmen were hurriedly heating the samovars.

He was gripped by an acute feeling of anxiety. He lay down, then got up and looked out of the window to see if the messenger was coming. But there was no one. He lay down again but got up again after half an hour, unable to control his anxiety, went out into the street and strode off towards the church.

The square near the fence was dark and deserted. Some soldiers were standing in a row at the top of the slope, saying nothing. They jumped when they saw Ryabovich and saluted. He acknowledged the salute and went down the familiar path.

The entire sky over the far bank was flooded with crimson; the moon was rising. Two peasant women were talking loudly and picking cabbage leaves as they walked along the edge of a kitchen garden. Beyond the gardens were some dark huts. On the near bank everything was much the same as in May: the path, the bushes, the willows overhanging the river . . . only there was no bold nightingale singing, no fragrant poplars or young grass. Ryabovich reached the garden and peered over the gate. It was dark and quiet and all he could see were the white trunks of the nearest birches and here and there little patches of avenue – everything else had merged into one black mass. Ryabovich looked hard, listened eagerly, and after standing and waiting for about a quarter of an hour, without hearing a sound or seeing a single light, he trudged wearily away . . .

He went down to the river, where he could see the general's bathing-hut and towels hanging over the rail on the little bridge. He went on to the bridge, stood for a moment and aimlessly fingered the towels. They felt cold and rough. He looked down at the water . . . the current was swift and purled, barely audibly, against the piles of the hut. The red moon was reflected in the water near the left bank; tiny waves rippled through the reflection, pulling it apart and breaking it up into little patches, as if trying to bear it away.

'How stupid, how very stupid!' Ryabovich thought as he looked at the fast-flowing water. Now, when he hoped for nothing, that adventure of the kiss, his impatience, his vague longings and disillusionment appeared in a new light. He didn't think it at all strange that he hadn't waited for the general's messenger or that he would never see the girl who had kissed him by mistake. On the contrary, he would have thought it strange if he *had* seen her . . .

The water raced past and he did not know where or why; it had flowed just as swiftly in May, when it grew from a little stream into a large river, flowed into the sea, evaporated and turned into rain. Perhaps this was the same water flowing past. To what purpose?

And the whole world, the whole of life, struck Ryabovich as a meaningless, futile joke. As he turned his eyes from the water to the sky, he remembered how fate had accidentally caressed him – in the guise of an unknown woman. He recalled the dreams and visions of that summer and his life seemed terribly empty, miserable, colourless . . . When he returned to his hut, none of the officers was there.

The batman reported that they had all gone to 'General Fontryabkin's' – he'd sent a messenger on horseback with the invitation. There was a brief flicker of joy in his heart, but he snuffed it out at once, lay on his bed and in defiance of fate – as though he wanted to bring its wrath down on his own head – he did not go to the general's.

The Two Volodyas

'Let me go, *I* want to drive. I'm going to sit next to the driver,' Sophia Lvovna shouted. 'Driver, wait. I'm coming up on to the box to sit next to you.'

She stood on the sledge while her husband Vladimir Nikitych and her childhood friend Vladimir Mikhaylych held her by the arm in case she fell. Away sped the troika.

'I said you shouldn't have given her brandy,' Vladimir Nikitych whispered irritably to his companion. 'You're a fine one!'

From past experience the Colonel knew that when women like his wife Sophia Lvovna had been in riotous, rather inebriated high spirits he could normally expect fits of hysterical laughter and tears to follow. He was afraid that once they got home he would have to run around with the cold compresses and medicine instead of being able to go to bed.

'Whoa!' Sophia Lvovna shouted. 'I want to drive.'

She was really very gay and in an exultant mood. For two months after her wedding she had been tormented by the thought that she had married Colonel Yagich for his money or, as they say, *par dépit*. That same evening, in the out-of-town restaurant, she finally became convinced that she loved him passionately. In spite of his fifty-four years, he was so trim, sprightly and athletic, and he told puns and joined in the gypsy girls' songs with such charm. It is true that nowadays old men are a thousand times more interesting than young ones, as though age and youth had changed places. The Colonel was two years older than her father, but was that important if, to be quite honest, he was infinitely stronger, more energetic and livelier than she was, even though she was only twenty-three?

'Oh, my darling!' she thought. 'My wonderful man!'

In the restaurant she had come to the conclusion too that not a spark remained of her old feelings. To her childhood friend Vladimir Mikhaylych, whom only yesterday she had loved to distraction, she now felt completely indifferent. The whole evening he had struck her as a lifeless, sleepy, boring nobody and the habitual coolness with which he avoided paying restaurant bills exasperated her so much this time that she very nearly told him, 'You should have stayed at home if you're so poor.' The Colonel footed the bill.

Perhaps it was the trees, telegraph poles and snowdrifts all flashing past that aroused the most varied thoughts. She reflected that the meal had cost one hundred and twenty roubles – with a hundred for the gypsies – and that the next day, if she so wished, she could throw a thousand roubles away, whereas two months ago, before the wedding, she did not have three roubles to call her own and she had to turn to her father for every little thing. How her life had changed!

Her thoughts were in a muddle and she remembered how, when she was about ten, Colonel Yagich, her husband now, had made advances to her aunt and how everyone in the house had said that he had ruined her. In fact, her aunt often came down to dinner with tear-stained eyes and was always going away somewhere; people said the poor woman was suffering terribly. In those days he was very handsome and had extraordinary success with women; the whole town knew him and he was said to visit his admirers every day, like a doctor doing his rounds. Even now, despite his grey hair, wrinkles and spectacles, his thin face looked handsome, especially in profile.

Sophia Lvovna's father was an army doctor and had once served in Yagich's regiment. Volodya senior's father had also been an army doctor and had once served in the same regiment as her own father and Yagich. Despite some highly involved and frantic amorous adventures Volodya junior had been an excellent student. He graduated with honours from university, had decided to specialize in foreign literature and was said to be writing his thesis. He lived in the barracks with his doctor father and he had no money of his own, although he was now thirty. When they were children, Sophia Lvovna and he had lived in different flats, but in the same building, and he often came to play with her; together they had dancing and French lessons. But when he grew up into a well-built, exceedingly good-looking young man, she began to be shy of him. Then she fell madly in love with him and was still in love until shortly before she married Yagich. He too had extraordinary success with women, from the age of fourteen almost, and the ladies who deceived their husbands with him exonerated themselves by saying Volodya was 'so little'. Not long before, he was said to be living in digs close to the university and every time you knocked, his footsteps could be heard on the other side of the door and then the whispered apology: '*Pardon, je ne suis pas seul.*' Yagich was delighted with him, gave him his blessing for the future as Derzhavin had blessed Pushkin, and was evidently very fond of him. For hours on end they would silently play billiards or piquet, and if Yagich went off somewhere in a troika, he would take Volodya with him; only Yagich shared the secret of his thesis. In earlier days, when the Colonel was younger, they were often rivals, but were never jealous of one another. When they were in company, which they frequented together, Yagich was called 'Big Volodya' and his friend 'Little Volodya'.

Besides Big Volodya and Little Volodya, and Sophia Lvovna, there was someone else in the sledge, Margarita Aleksandrovna – or Rita as everyone called her – Mrs Yagich's cousin. She was a spinster, in her thirties, very pale, with black eyebrows, pince-nez, who chain-smoked even when it was freezing; there was always ash on her lap and chest. She spoke through her nose and drawled; she was cold and unemotional, could drink any quantity of liqueur or brandy without getting drunk and told stories abounding in *doubles entendres* in a dull, tasteless way. At home she read the learned reviews all day long, scattering ash all over them; or she would eat crystallized apples.

'Sophia, don't play the fool,' she drawled; 'it's really so stupid.'

When the town gates came into view the troika slowed down; they caught glimpses of people and houses, and Sophia quietened down, snuggled against her husband and gave herself up to her thoughts. And now gloomy thoughts began to mingle with her happy, carefree fantasies. The man opposite knew that she had loved him (so she thought), and of course he believed the reports that she had married the

Colonel *par dépit*. Not once had she confessed her love and she did not want him to know. She had concealed her feelings, but his expression clearly showed that he understood her perfectly, and so her pride suffered. But most humiliating of all about her situation was the fact that Little Volodya had suddenly started paying attention to her after her marriage, which had never happened before. He would sit with her for hours on end, in silence, or telling her some nonsense; and now in the sledge he was gently touching her leg or squeezing her hand, without saying a word. Evidently, all he wanted was for her to get married. No less obviously, he did not think much of her and she interested him only in a certain way, as an immoral, disreputable woman. And this mingling of triumphant love for her husband and injured pride was the reason for her behaving so irresponsibly, prompting her to sit on the box and shout and whistle . . .

Just as they were passing the convent the great twenty-ton bell started clanging away. Rita crossed herself.

'Our Olga is in that convent,' Sophia Lvovna said, crossing herself and shuddering.

'Why did she become a nun?' the Colonel asked.

'*Par dépit*,' Rita answered angrily, obviously hinting at Sophia Lvovna's marriage to Yagich. 'This *par dépit* is all the rage now. It's a challenge to the whole of society. She was a proper good-time girl, a terrible flirt, all she liked was dances and dancing partners. And then suddenly we have all this! She took us all by surprise!'

'That's not true,' Little Volodya said, lowering the collar of his fur coat and revealing his handsome face. 'This wasn't a case of *par dépit*, but something really terrible. Her brother

Dmitry was sentenced to hard labour in Siberia and no one knows where he is now. The mother died of grief.' He raised his collar again. 'And Olga did the right thing,' he added dully. 'Living as a ward, and with a treasure like our Sophia Lvovna, what's more – that's enough food for thought!'

Sophia Lvovna noted the contempt in his voice and wanted to say something very nasty in reply, but she said nothing. Once more euphoria gripped her. She stood up and shouted tearfully, 'I want to go to morning service. Driver, turn back! I want to see Olga!'

They turned back. The convent bell had a dull peal and Sophia Lvovna felt there was something in it reminding her of Olga and her life. Bells rang out from other churches. When the driver had brought the troika to a halt, Sophia leapt from the sledge and rushed unescorted to the gates.

'Please don't be long!' her husband shouted. 'It's late.'

She went through the dark gates, then along the path leading to the main church; the light snow crunched under her feet and the tolling of the bells sounded right over her head now and seemed to penetrate her whole being. First she came to the church door, the three steps down, then the porch, with paintings of the saints on both sides; there was a smell of juniper and incense. Then came another door, which a dark figure opened, bowing very low . . . In the church the service had not yet begun. One of the nuns was in front of the icon-screen lighting candles in their holders, another was lighting a chandelier. Here and there, close to the columns and side-chapels, were motionless, black figures. 'They'll be standing in exactly the same places till morning,' Sophia Lvovna thought and the whole place struck her as dark, cold, depressing – more depressing than a graveyard. Feeling bored, she glanced at the motionless, frozen figures and suddenly her heart sank. Somehow she recognized one of the nuns – short, with thin shoulders and a black shawl on her head – as Olga, although when she had entered the convent she had been plump and taller, she thought. Deeply disturbed for some reason, Sophia Lvovna hesitantly walked over to the lay sister, looked over her shoulder into her face and saw it *was* Olga.

'Olga!' she said, clasping her hands and too excited to say anything else. 'Olga!'

The nun recognized her immediately, raised her eyebrows in astonishment and her pale, freshly washed face (even, it seemed, her white kerchief visible under her shawl) glowed with joy.

'God has performed a miracle,' she said and also clasped her thin, pale little hands.

Sophia Lvovna firmly embraced her and kissed her, frightened as she did so that her breath might smell of drink.

'We were just passing and we thought of you,' she said breathlessly, as though she had just completed a fast walk. 'Heavens, how pale you are! I'm . . . I'm very pleased to see you. Well, how are you? Bored?' Sophia Lvovna looked round at the other nuns and now she lowered her voice: 'So much has happened . . . you know I married Volodya Yagich. You must remember him . . . I'm very happy.'

'Well, thank the Lord for that! And is your father well?'

'Yes, he often remembers you. But you must come and see us during the holidays, Olga. Will you do that?'

'Yes, I'll come,' Olga said smiling. 'I'll come the day after tomorrow.'

Without even knowing why, Sophia burst into tears and cried in silence for a whole minute. Then she dried her eyes and said, 'Rita will be very sorry she didn't see you. She's with us too. And Little Volodya. They're at the gate. How pleased they would be to see you! Come out and see them, the service hasn't started yet.'

'All right,' Olga agreed. She crossed herself three times and walked out with Sophia Lvovna.

'So, you said you're happy, Sophia,' she said after they were past the gates.

'Very.'

'Well, thank God.'

When Big Volodya and Little Volodya saw the nun they got off the sledge and greeted her respectfully. They were visibly moved by her pale face and her nun's black habit, and they were both pleased that she remembered them and had come to greet them. Sophia Lvovna wrapped her in a rug and covered her with one flap of her fur coat to protect her from the cold. Her recent tears had lightened and cleansed her soul and she was glad that the noisy, riotous and essentially immoral night had unexpectedly come to such a pure and quiet conclusion. Then to keep Olga by her side longer, she suggested, 'Let's take her for a ride! Olga, get in. Just a little one.'

The men expected the nun to refuse – religious people don't go around in troikas – but to their amazement she agreed and got in. When the troika hurtled off towards the town gates, no one said a word; their only concern was to make her warm and comfortable. Each one of them thought about the difference in her from before. Her face was impassive, somewhat expressionless, cold, pale, transparent, as though water flowed in her veins instead of blood. Two or three years ago she had been buxom and rosy-cheeked, had talked about eligible bachelors and laughed loud at the least thing.

The troika turned round at the town gates. Ten minutes later they were back at the convent and Olga climbed out. The bells were ringing a series of chimes.

'God be with you,' Olga said, giving a low, nun-like bow.

'So you will come then, Olga?'

'Of course I will.'

She quickly left and soon disappeared through the dark gateway. After the troika had moved on everyone somehow felt very sad. No one said a word. Sophia Lvovna felt weak all over and her heart sank. Making a nun get into a sledge and go for a ride with that drunken crowd struck her now as stupid, tactless and almost sacrilegious. The desire for self-deception vanished with her tipsiness and now she clearly realized that she did not and could not love her husband, it was all nothing but silly nonsense. She had married for money because, as her ex-schoolgirl friends put it, he was 'madly rich', because she was terrified of becoming an old maid, like Rita, because her doctor father got on her nerves and because she wanted to annoy Little Volodya. Had she guessed when she was contemplating marriage that it would turn out to be so nasty, painful and ugly, she would never have agreed to it, not for anything in the world. But the damage was done now, she had to accept things.

They arrived home. As she lay in her warm, soft bed and covered herself with a blanket, Sophia Lvovna recalled the dark porch, the smell of incense, the figures by the columns, and she was distressed at the thought that these figures would still be standing there, quite motionless, all the time she was sleeping. Early morning service would be interminably long, and after that there would be the hours, then Mass, then more prayers . . .

'But surely God exists? He certainly exists and I must certainly die. Therefore, sooner or later, I must think of my soul, eternal life, like Olga does. Olga is saved now, she has solved all her problems for herself . . . But what if there is *no* God? Then her life has been wasted. But how has it been wasted? Why?'

A minute later another thought entered her head. 'God exists, death will certainly come. I should be thinking of my soul. If Olga could see her death this very minute she would not be afraid. She's ready. But the most important thing is, she's solved the riddle of existence for herself. God exists . . . yes. But isn't there another way out apart from becoming a nun? *That* means renouncing life, destroying it . . .' Sophia Lvovna became rather scared and hid her head under the pillow. 'I mustn't think about it,' she whispered, 'I mustn't.'

Yagich was walking up and down in the next room, his spurs softly jingling; he was deep in thought. Sophia Lvovna thought that this man was near and dear to her only in one thing – he was called Volodya too. She sat on her bed and tenderly called, 'Volodya!'

'What do you want?' her husband replied.

'Nothing.'

She lay down again. There were bells tolling – from that same convent, perhaps – and once again she recalled the porch and the dark figures. Thoughts of God and inescapable death wandered through her mind; she pulled the blanket over her head to drown the sound of the bells. She expected, before old age and death came, that her life would drag on for such a terribly long time, and from one day to the next she would have to cope with the nearness of someone she did not love, and who had come into the room just at that moment and was getting into bed; and she would have to suppress that hopeless love for another – someone who was so young, so charming and apparently so unusual. She looked at her husband and wanted to say good night, but she suddenly burst into tears instead. She felt annoyed with herself.

'Well, we're off again,' Yagich said.

She did calm down, but not until later, towards ten in the morning. She had stopped crying and shaking all over; she developed a severe headache, however. Yagich was hurrying, getting ready for late Mass and in the next room he was grumbling at the batman helping him dress. He came into the bedroom once, his spurs softly jingling, took something, and when he came in a second time he was wearing epaulettes and decorations; he limped slightly from rheumatism. He gave Sophia Lvovna the impression he was a beast of prey, prowling and looking round.

Then she heard him on the telephone. 'Please put me through to the Vasilyevsky Barracks,' he said. A minute later he went on, 'Is that Vasilyevsky Barracks? Please ask Dr Salimovich to come to the phone.' Then, a minute later, 'Who am I speaking to? Volodya? Fine. My dear chap, please ask your father to come over right away, my wife is terribly off colour after what happened yesterday. What's that? He's out? Hm . . . thanks . . . Yes, I'd be much obliged. *Merci.*'

Yagich came into the bedroom for the third time, bent over his wife, made the sign of the cross over her, let her kiss his hand (women who loved him would kiss his hand, he was used to this), and said he would be back for dinner. And he left.

Towards noon the maid announced Little Volodya. Swaying from weariness and her headache, Sophia Lvovna quickly put on her stunning new lilac, fur-trimmed negligee and hurriedly tidied her hair. In her heart she felt inexpressibly tender and trembled for joy – and for fear he might leave. She wanted just one look at him.

Little Volodya was paying her a visit in formal dress – tailcoat and white tie. When Sophia Lvovna came into the drawing-room he kissed her hand, said how deeply sorry he was to see her so unwell. When they had sat down he praised her negligee.

'Seeing Olga last night has upset me,' she said. 'At first it was painful for me, but now I envy her. She is like an immovable rock, it's impossible to budge her. But was there really no other way out for her, Volodya? Can burying oneself alive really solve life's problems? You'd call that death, not life, wouldn't you?' At the mention of Olga, Little Volodya's face showed deep emotion. 'Now look, Volodya, you're a clever man,' Sophia Lvovna said. 'Teach me to be like her. Of course, I'm a non-believer and I couldn't become a nun. But couldn't I do something that would be just as good? I find life hard enough.' After a brief silence she continued, 'Teach me . . . tell me something that will convince me. Just one word.'

'One word? Okay. Ta-ra-ra-boomdeay.'

'Volodya, why do you despise me?' she asked excitedly. 'You speak to me in some special – if you'll forgive the expression – fancy language that one doesn't use with friends and respectable women. You're a successful scholar, you love your studies, but why do you never tell me about them? Why? Aren't I good enough?'

Little Volodya frowned irritably and said, 'Why this sudden passion for scholarship? Perhaps you want us to have a constitution? Or perhaps sturgeon with horseradish?'

'Oh, have it your way then. I'm a mediocre, worthless, unprincipled, stupid woman . . . I've made thousands, thousands of mistakes. I'm not right in the head, a loose woman, and for that I deserve contempt. But you're ten years older than me, Volodya, aren't you? And my husband is thirty years older. You watched me grow up and if you'd wanted to, you could have made me anything you wanted, an angel even. But you . . .' (here her voice shook) 'treat me dreadfully. Yagich was an old man when he married me, and you . . .'

'Well, enough of that. Enough,' Volodya said, drawing closer to her and kissing both her hands. 'We'll leave the Schopenhauers to philosophize and argue about anything they like, but now we're going to kiss these sweet little hands.'

'You despise me and if only you knew the suffering it causes me,' she said hesitantly, knowing beforehand that he would not believe her. 'If you only knew how I want to improve myself, to start a new life! It fills me with joy just thinking about it,' she murmured and actually shed a few joyous tears. 'To be a good, honest, decent person, not to lie, to have a purpose in life.'

'Stop it please! You don't have to put on an act for me, I don't like it,' Volodya said, looking peevish. 'Heavens, you'd think we were at the theatre! Let's behave like normal human beings!'

To prevent him from leaving in a temper she began to make excuses, forced herself to smile – to please him – mentioned Olga again and that she wanted to solve the riddle of her existence, to become a real human being.

'Ta-ra-ra-boomdeay,' he chanted softly. 'Ta-ra-ra-boomdeay!'

And then quite suddenly he clasped her waist. Barely conscious of what she was doing she put her hands on his shoulders and for a whole minute looked rapturously at his clever, sarcastic face, his forehead, eyes, handsome beard . . .

'You've known for a long time that I love you,' she confessed with an agonized blush and she felt that even her lips had twisted in a paroxysm of shame. 'I love you. So why do you torment me?'

She closed her eyes and kissed him firmly on the lips. For a long time – a whole minute perhaps – she just could not bring herself to end this kiss, although she knew very well that she was behaving badly, that he might tell her off, or that a servant might come in . . .

Half an hour later, when he had got what he wanted, he sat in the dining-room eating a snack while she knelt before him, staring hungrily into his face. He told her she was like a small dog waiting for someone to toss it a piece of ham. Then he sat her on one knee, rocked her like a child and sang, 'Ta-ra-ra-boomdeay . . . Ta-ra-ra-boomdeay!'

When he was about to leave she asked him passionately, 'When? Later on? Where?' And she held out both hands to his mouth, as if wanting to catch his reply in them.

'It's not really convenient today,' he said after a moment's thought. 'Perhaps tomorrow, though.'

And they parted. Before lunch Sophia Lvovna went off to the convent to see Olga, but was told that she was reading the Psalter for someone who had died. From the convent she went to her father's and drove aimlessly up and down the main streets and side-streets until evening. While she was riding, for some reason she kept remembering that aunt with the tear-stained eyes, who was fretting her life away.

That night they all went riding on troikas again and heard the gypsies in that out-of-town restaurant. And when they were once again passing the convent Sophia Lvovna thought of Olga and became terrified at the thought that there was no escape for girls and women in her circle, except perpetual troika-rides or entering a convent to mortify the flesh . . .

The following day she had a lovers' rendezvous once again. She went for solitary cab-rides around town and thought of her aunt.

A week later Little Volodya dropped her. Then life reverted to normal and was just as boring, dreary – and sometimes just as excruciating as it had ever been. The Colonel and Little Volodya had long billiards and piquet sessions, Rita told her tasteless anecdotes in the same lifeless fashion,

Sophia Lvovna kept driving in cabs and asking her husband to take her for troika-rides.

Almost every day she called at the convent, boring Olga with her complaints of intolerable suffering; she cried and felt that she had brought something impure, pathetic and shabby into the cell. Olga, however, as if repeating a well-learnt lesson parrot-fashion, told her that there was nothing to worry about, that it would all pass and that God would forgive her.

Gooseberries

The sky had been overcast with rain clouds since early morning. The weather was mild, and not hot and oppressive as it can be on dull grey days when storm clouds lie over the fields for ages and you wait for rain which never comes. Ivan Ivanych, the vet, and Burkin, a teacher at the high school, were tired of walking and thought they would never come to the end of the fields. They could just make out the windmills at the village of Mironositskoye in the far distance – a range of hills stretched away to the right and disappeared far beyond it. They both knew that the river was there, with meadows, green willows and farmsteads, and that if they climbed one of the hills they would see yet another vast expanse of fields, telegraph wires and a train resembling a caterpillar in the distance. In fine weather they could see even as far as the town. And now, in calm weather, when the whole of nature had become gentle and dreamy, Ivan Ivanych and Burkin were filled with love for those open spaces and they both thought what a vast and beautiful country it was.

'Last time we were in Elder Prokofy's barn, you were going to tell me a story,' Burkin said.

'Yes, I wanted to tell you about my brother.'

Ivan Ivanych heaved a long sigh and lit his pipe before beginning his narrative; but at that moment down came the rain. Five minutes later it was simply teeming. Ivan Ivanych and Burkin were in two minds as to what they should do. The dogs were already soaked through and stood with their tails drooping, looking at them affectionately.

'We must take shelter,' Burkin said. 'Let's go to Alyokhin's, it's not very far.'

'All right, let's go there.'

They changed direction and went across mown fields, walking straight on at first, and then bearing right until they came out on the high road. Before long, poplars, a garden, then the red roofs of barns came into view. The river glinted, and then they caught sight of a wide stretch of water and a white bathing-hut. This was Sofino, where Alyokhin lived.

The mill was turning and drowned the noise of the rain. The wall of the dam shook. Wet horses with downcast heads were standing by some carts and peasants went around with sacks on their heads. Everything was damp, muddy and bleak, and the water had a cold, malevolent look. Ivan Ivanych and Burkin felt wet, dirty and terribly uncomfortable. Their feet were weighed down by mud and when they crossed the dam and walked up to the barns near the manor house they did not say a word and seemed to be angry with each other.

A winnowing fan was droning away in one of the barns and dust poured out of the open door. On the threshold stood the master himself, Alyokhin, a man of about forty, tall, stout, with long hair, and he looked more like a professor or an artist than a landowner. He wore a white shirt that hadn't been washed for a very long time, and it was tied round with a piece of rope as a belt. Instead of trousers he was wearing underpants; mud and straw clung to his boots. His nose and eyes were black with dust. He immediately recognized Ivan Ivanych and Burkin, and was clearly delighted to see them.

'Please come into the house, gentlemen,' he said, smiling, 'I'll be with you in a jiffy.'

It was a large house, with two storeys. Alyokhin lived on the ground floor in the two rooms with vaulted ceilings and small windows where his estate managers used to live. They were simply furnished and smelled of rye bread, cheap vodka and harness. He seldom used the main rooms upstairs, reserving them for guests. Ivan Ivanych and Burkin were welcomed by the maid, who was such a beautiful young woman that they both stopped and stared at each other.

'You can't imagine how glad I am to see you, gentlemen,' Alyokhin said as he followed them into the hall. 'A real surprise!' Then he turned to the maid and said, 'Pelageya, bring some dry clothes for the gentlemen. I suppose I'd better change too. But I must have a wash first, or you'll think I haven't had one since spring. Would you like to come to the bathing-hut while they get things ready in the house?'

The beautiful Pelageya, who had such a dainty look and gentle face, brought soap and towels, and Alyokhin went off with his guests to the bathing-hut.

'Yes, it's ages since I had a good wash,' he said as he undressed. 'As you can see, it's a nice hut. My father built it, but I never find time these days for a swim.'

He sat on one of the steps and smothered his long hair and neck with soap; the water turned brown.

'Yes, I must confess . . .' Ivan Ivanych muttered, with a meaningful look at his head.

'Haven't had a wash for ages,' Alyokhin repeated in his embarrassment and soaped himself again; the water turned a dark inky blue.

Ivan Ivanych came out of the cabin, dived in with a loud splash and swam in the rain, making broad sweeps with his arms and sending out waves with white lilies bobbing about on them. He swam right out to the middle of the reach and dived. A moment later he popped up somewhere else and swam on, continually trying to dive right to the bottom.

'Oh, good God,' he kept saying with great relish. 'Good God . . .'

He reached the mill, said a few words to the peasants, then he turned and floated on his back in the middle with his face under the rain. Burkin and Alyokhin were already dressed and ready to leave, but he kept on swimming and diving.

'Oh, dear God,' he said. 'Oh, God!'

'Now that's enough,' Burkin shouted.

They went back to the house. Only when the lamp in the large upstairs drawing-room was alight and Burkin and Ivan Ivanych, wearing silk dressing-gowns and warm slippers, were sitting in armchairs and Alyokhin, washed and combed now and with a new frock-coat on, was walking up and down, obviously savouring the warmth, cleanliness, dry clothes and light shoes, while his beautiful Pelageya glided silently over the carpet and gently smiled as she served tea and jam on a tray – only then did Ivan Ivanych begin his story. It seemed that Burkin and Alyokhin were not the only ones who were listening, but also the ladies (young and old) and the officers, who were looking down calmly and solemnly from their gilt frames on the walls.

'There are two of us brothers,' he began, 'myself – Ivan Ivanych – and Nikolay Ivanych, who's two years younger. I studied to be a vet, while Nikolay worked in the district tax office from the time he was nineteen. Chimsha-Gimalaysky, our father, had served as a private, but when he was promoted to officer we became hereditary gentlemen and owners of a small estate. After he died, this estate was sequestrated to pay off his debts, but despite this we spent our boyhood in the country free to do what we wanted. Just like any other village children, we stayed out in the fields and woods for days and nights, minded horses, stripped bark, went fishing, and so on . . . As you know very well, anyone who has ever caught a ruff or watched migrating thrushes swarming over his native village on cool clear autumn days can never live in a town afterwards and he'll always hanker after the free and open life until his dying day. My brother was miserable in the tax office. The years passed, but there he stayed, always at the same old desk, copying out the same old documents and obsessed with this longing for the country. And gradually this longing took the form of a definite wish, a dream of buying a nice little estate somewhere in the country, beside a river or a lake.

'He was a kind, gentle man and I was very fond of him, but I could never feel any sympathy for him in this longing to lock himself away in a country house for the rest of his life. They say a man needs only six feet of earth, but surely they must mean a corpse – not a *man*! These days they seem to think that it's very good if our educated classes want to go back to the land and set their hearts on a country estate. But in reality these estates are only that same six feet all over again. To leave the town and all its noise and hubbub, to go and shut yourself away on your little estate – that's no life! It's selfishness, laziness, a peculiar brand of monasticism that achieves nothing. A man needs more than six feet of earth and a little place in the country, he needs the whole wide world, the whole of nature, where there's room for him to display his potential, all the manifold attributes of his free spirit.

'As he sat there in his office, my brother Nikolay dreamt of soup made from his own home-grown cabbages, soup that would fill the whole house with a delicious smell; eating meals on the green grass; sleeping in the sun; sitting on a bench outside the main gates for hours on end and looking at the fields and woods. Booklets on agriculture and words of wisdom from calendars were his joy, his favourite spiritual nourishment. He liked newspapers as well, but he only read property adverts – for so many acres of arable land and meadows, with "house, river, garden, mill, and ponds fed by running springs". And he had visions of garden paths, flowers, fruit, nesting-boxes for starlings, ponds teeming with carp – you know the kind of thing. These visions varied according to the adverts he happened to see, but for some reason, in every single one, there *had* to be gooseberry bushes. "Life in the country has its comforts," he used to say. "You can sit drinking tea on your balcony, while your ducks are swimming in the pond . . . it all smells so good and um . . . there's your gooseberries growing away!"

'He drew up a plan for his estate and it turned out exactly

the same every time: (a) manor house; (b) servants' quarters; (c) kitchen garden; (d) gooseberry bushes. He lived a frugal life, economizing on food and drink, dressing any-old-how – just like a beggar – and putting every penny he saved straight into the bank. He was terribly mean. It was really painful to look at him, so I used to send him a little money on special occasions. But he would put that in the bank too. Once a man has his mind firmly made up there's nothing you can do about it.

'Years passed and he was transferred to another province. He was now in his forties, still reading newspaper adverts and still saving up. Then I heard that he'd got married. So that he could buy a country estate with gooseberry bushes, he married an ugly old widow, for whom he felt nothing and only because she had a little money tucked away. He made her life miserable too, half-starved her and banked her money into his own account. She'd been married to a postmaster and was used to pies and fruit liqueurs, but with her second husband she didn't even have enough black bread. This kind of life made her wither away, and within three years she'd gone to join her maker. Of course, my brother didn't think that *he* was to blame – not for one minute! Like vodka, money can make a man do the most peculiar things. There was once a merchant living in our town who was on his deathbed. Just before he died, he asked for some honey, stirred it up with all his money and winning lottery tickets, and swallowed the lot to stop anyone else from laying their hands on it. And another time, when I was inspecting cattle at some railway station, a dealer fell under a train and had his leg cut off. We took him to the local casualty department.

The blood simply gushed out, a terrible sight, but all he did was ask for his leg back and was only bothered about the twenty roubles he had tucked away in the boot. Scared he might lose them, I dare say!'

'But that's neither here nor there,' Burkin said.

'When his wife died,' Ivan continued, after a pause for thought, 'my brother started looking for an estate. Of course, you can look around for five years and still make the wrong choice and you finish up with something you never even dreamt of. So brother Nikolay bought about three hundred acres, with manor house, servants' quarters and a park, on a mortgage through an estate agent. But there wasn't any orchard, gooseberries or duck pond. There *was* a river, but the water was always the colour of coffee because of the brickworks on one side of the estate and a bone-ash factory on the other. But my dear Nikolay didn't seem to care. He ordered twenty gooseberry bushes, planted them out and settled down to a landowner's life.

'Last year I visited him, as I wanted to see what was going on. In his letter my brother had called his estate "Chumbaroklov Patch" or "Gimalaysky's". One afternoon I turned up at "Gimalaysky's". It was a hot day. Everywhere there were ditches, fences, hedges, rows of small fir trees and there seemed no way into the yard or anywhere to leave my horse. I went up to the house, only to be welcomed by a fat ginger dog that looked rather like a pig. It wanted to bark, but it was too lazy. Then a barefooted, plump cook – she resembled a pig as well – came out of the kitchen and told me the master was having his after-lunch nap. So I went to my brother's room and there he was sitting up in bed with a blanket over his knees. He'd aged, put on weight and looked very flabby. His cheeks, nose and lips stuck out and I thought any moment he was going to grunt into his blanket, like a pig.

'We embraced and wept for joy, and at the sad thought that once we were young and now both of us were grey, and that our lives were nearly over. He got dressed and led me on a tour of the estate.

' "Well, how's it going?" I asked.

' "All right, thank God. It's a good life."

'No longer was he the poor, timid little clerk of before, but a real squire, a *gentleman*. He felt quite at home, being used to country life by then and he was enjoying himself. He ate a great deal, took proper baths, and he was putting on weight. Already he was suing the district council and both factories, and he got very peeved when the villagers didn't call him "sir". He paid great attention to his spiritual well-being (as a gentleman should) and he couldn't dispense charity nice and quietly, but had to make a great show of it. And what did it all add up to? He doled out bicarbonate of soda or castor oil to his villagers – regardless of what they were suffering from – and on his name-day held a thanksgiving service in the village, supplying vodka in plenty, as he thought this was the right thing to do. Oh, those horrid pints of vodka! Nowadays your fat squire drags his villagers off to court for letting their cattle stray on his land and the very next day (if it's a high holiday) stands them all a few pints of vodka. They'll drink it, shout hurray and fall at his feet in a drunken stupor. Better standards of living, plenty to eat, idleness – all this makes us Russians terribly smug. Back in his office, Nikolay had been too scared even to voice any opinions of his own, but now he was expounding the eternal verities in true ministerial style: "Education is essential, but premature as far as the common people are concerned" or "Corporal punishment, generally speaking, is harmful, but in certain cases it can be useful and irreplaceable". And he'd say, "I know the working classes and how to handle them. They *like* me, I only have to lift my little finger and they'll do *anything* for me."

'And he said all this, mark you, with a clever, good-natured smile. Time after time he'd say "we *gentlemen*" or "speaking as *one of the gentry*". He'd evidently forgotten that our grandfather had been a peasant and our father a common soldier. Even our absolutely ridiculous surname, Chimsha-Gimalaysky, was melodious, distinguished and highly agreeable to his ears now.

'But it's myself I'm concerned with, not him. I'd like to tell you about the change that came over me during the few hours I spent on his estate. Later, when we were having tea, his cook brought us a plateful of gooseberries. They weren't shop gooseberries, but home-grown, the first fruits of the bushes he'd planted. Nikolay laughed and stared at them for a whole minute, with tears in his eyes. He was too deeply moved for words. Then he popped one in his mouth, looked at me like an enraptured child that has finally been given a long-awaited toy and said, "Absolutely delicious!" He ate some greedily and kept repeating, "So tasty, you *must* try one!"

'They were hard and sour, but as Pushkin says: "Uplifting illusion is dearer to us than a host of truths." This was a happy man whose cherished dreams had clearly come true, who had achieved his life's purpose, had got what he wanted and was happy with his lot – and himself. My thoughts about human happiness, for some peculiar reason, had always been tinged with a certain sadness. But now, seeing this happy man, I was overwhelmed by a feeling of despondency that was close to utter despair. I felt particularly low that night. They made up a bed for me in the room next to my brother's. He was wide awake and I could hear him getting up, going over to the plate and helping himself to one gooseberry at a time. And I thought how many satisfied, happy people really do exist in this world! And what a powerful force they are! Just take a look at this life of ours and you will see the arrogance and idleness of the strong, the ignorance and bestiality of the weak. Everywhere there's unspeakable poverty, overcrowding, degeneracy, drunkenness, hypocrisy and stupid lies . . . And yet peace and quiet reign in every house and street. Out of fifty thousand people you won't find one who is prepared to shout out loud and make a strong protest. We see people buying food in the market, eating during the day, sleeping at night-time, talking nonsense, marrying, growing old and then contentedly carting their dead off to the cemetery. But we don't hear or see those who suffer: the real tragedies of life are enacted somewhere behind the scenes. Everything is calm and peaceful and the only protest comes from statistics – and they can't talk. Figures show that so many went mad, so many bottles of vodka were emptied, so many children died from malnutrition. And clearly this kind of system is what people need. It's obvious that the happy man feels contented only because the unhappy ones bear their burden without saying a word: if it weren't for their silence, happiness would be quite impossible. It's a kind of mass hypnosis. Someone ought to stand with a hammer at the door of every happy contented man, continually banging on it to remind him that there are unhappy people around and that however happy *he* may be at the time, sooner or later life will show him its claws and disaster will overtake him in the form of illness, poverty, bereavement and there will be no one to hear or see him. But there isn't anyone holding a hammer, so our happy man goes his own sweet way and is only gently ruffled by life's trivial cares, as an aspen is ruffled by the breeze. All's well as far as *he's* concerned.

'That night I realized that I too was happy and contented,' Ivan Ivanych went on, getting to his feet. 'I too had lectured people over dinner – or out hunting – on how to live, on what to believe, on how to handle the common people. And I too had told them that knowledge is a shining lamp, that education is essential, and that plain reading and writing is good enough for the masses, for the moment. Freedom is a blessing, I told them, and we need it like the air we breathe, but we must wait for it patiently.'

Ivan Ivanych turned to Burkin and said angrily, 'Yes, that's what I used to say and now I'd like to know *what* is it we're waiting for? I'm asking you, *what*? What is it we're trying to prove? I'm told that nothing can be achieved in five minutes, that it takes time for any kind of idea to be realized; it's a gradual process. But who says so? And what is there to prove he's right? You refer to the natural order of things, to the law of cause and effect. But *is* there any law or order in a state of affairs where a lively, thinking person like myself should have to stand by a ditch and wait until it's choked with weeds, or silted up, when I could quite easily, perhaps, leap across it or bridge it? I ask you again, what are we waiting for? Until we have no more strength to live, although we long to and *need* to go on living?

'I left my brother early next morning and ever since then I've found town life unbearable. I'm depressed by peace and quiet, I'm scared of peering through windows, nothing makes me more dejected than the sight of a happy family sitting round the table drinking tea. But I'm old now, no longer fit for the fray, I'm even incapable of hating. I only feel sick at heart, irritable and exasperated. At night my head seems to be on fire with so many thoughts crowding in and I can't get any sleep . . . Oh, if only I were young again!'

Ivan Ivanych paced the room excitedly, repeating, 'If only I were young again!'

Suddenly he went up to Alyokhin and squeezed one hand, then the other. 'Pavel Konstantinych,' he pleaded, 'don't go to sleep or be lulled into complacency! While you're still young, strong and healthy, never stop doing good! Happiness doesn't exist, we don't need any such thing. If life has *any* meaning or purpose, you won't find it in happiness, but in something more rational, in something greater. Doing good!'

Ivan Ivanych said all this with a pitiful, imploring smile, as though pleading for himself.

Afterwards all three of them sat in armchairs in different parts of the room and said nothing. Ivan Ivanych's story satisfied neither Burkin nor Alyokhin. It was boring listening to that story about some poor devil of a clerk who ate gooseberries, while those generals and ladies, who seemed to have come to life in the gathering gloom, peered out of their gilt frames. For some reason they would have preferred discussing and hearing about refined people, about ladies. The fact that they were all sitting in a drawing-room where everything – the draped chandeliers, the armchairs, the carpets underfoot – indicated that those same people who were now looking out of their frames had once walked around, sat down and drunk their tea there . . . and with beautiful Pelageya moving about here without a sound – all this was better than any story.

Alyokhin was dying to get to bed. That morning he had been up and about very early (before three) working on the farm, and he could hardly keep his eyes open. However, he was frightened he might miss some interesting story if he left now, so he stayed. He didn't even try to fathom if everything that Ivan Ivanych had just been saying was clever, or even true: he was only too glad that his guests did not discuss oats or hay or tar, but things that had nothing to do with his way of life, and he wanted them to continue . . .

'But it's time we got some sleep,' Burkin said, standing up. 'May I wish you all a very good night!'

Alyokhin bade them good night and went down to his room, while his guests stayed upstairs. They had been given the large room with two old, elaborately carved beds and an ivory crucifix in one corner. These wide, cool beds had been made by the beautiful Pelageya and the linen had a pleasant fresh smell.

Ivan Ivanych undressed without a word and got into bed.

Then he muttered, 'Lord have mercy on us sinners!' and pulled the blankets over his head. His pipe, which was lying on a table, smelt strongly of stale tobacco and Burkin was so puzzled as to where the terrible smell was coming from that it was a long time before he fell asleep.

All night long the rain beat against the windows.

Penguin Little Black Classics Vol. I

01. GIOVANNI BOCCACCIO

Mrs Rosie and the Priest

02. EDGAR ALLAN POE

The Tell-Tale Heart

03. ANTON CHEKHOV

Gooseberries

04. LEO TOLSTOY

How Much Land Does a Man Need?

05. GUSTAVE FLAUBERT

A Simple Heart

06. RYUNOSUKE AKUTAGAWA

The Life of a Stupid Man

07. THOMAS HARDY

The Withered Arm

08. KENKO

A Cup of Sake Beneath the Cherry Trees

09. WILLIAM BLAKE

Tyger Tyger

10. RAINER MARIA RILKE

Letters to a Young Poet

企鹅经典：小黑书　第一辑

01. 贝尔科洛蕾夫人与神父

［意］薄伽丘

02. 泄密的心

［美］爱伦 · 坡

03. 醋栗

［俄］契诃夫

04. 一个人需要许多土地吗？

［俄］列夫 · 托尔斯泰

05. 一颗简单的心

［法］福楼拜

06. 傻子的一生

［日］芥川龙之介

07. 萎缩的胳膊

［英］托马斯 · 哈代

08. 樱花树下的清酒

［日］吉田兼好

09. 虎！虎！

［英］威廉 · 布莱克

10. 给一个青年诗人的十封信

［奥］里尔克

“‘哎呀，
我的上帝啊！……’
他反复说着，
‘游得痛快极了。
哎呀，
我的上帝啊！……’”

PENGUIN

LITTLE BLACK

CLASSICS

*此中文译本译自俄语原文

醋栗

Gooseberries

[俄] 契诃夫 著

汝龙 译

中信出版集团 · 北京

图书在版编目（C I P）数据

企鹅经典 · 小黑书 . 第一辑 : 英、汉 / (日) 吉田兼好等著 ; 文东等译 . -- 北京 : 中信出版社 , 2018.11 (2022.7 重印)
书名原文 : Penguin Little Black Classics
ISBN 978-7-5086-9400-9

Ⅰ . ①企… Ⅱ . ①吉… ②文… Ⅲ . ①世界文学—作品综合集—英、汉 Ⅳ . ① I11

中国版本图书馆 CIP 数据核字 (2018) 第 193780 号

Gooseberries
'The Kiss' was first published in 1887; 'The Two Volodyas' in 1893; and 'Gooseberries' in 1898. This selection has been taken from the three volumes of Chekhov's short stories available in Penguin Classics. This selection published in Penguin Classics 2015.

企鹅经典：小黑书　第一辑
醋栗

著　　者：[俄] 契诃夫
译　　者：汝 龙
出版发行：中信出版集团股份有限公司
（北京市朝阳区惠新东街甲 4 号富盛大厦 2 座 邮编 100029）
承 印 者：河北鹏润印刷有限公司

开　　本：787mm×1092mm　1/32　　印　　张：41　　字　　数：300 千字
版　　次：2018 年 11 月第 1 版　　印　　次：2022 年 7 月第13次印刷
京权图字：01-2018-6477
书　　号：ISBN 978-7-5086-9400-9
定　　价：149.00 元（全 10 册）

服务热线：400-600-8099
投稿邮箱：author@citicpub.com

目录

吻

五月二十日傍晚八点钟，某炮兵后备旅的所有六个连，到露营地去的途中，在梅斯捷奇金村停下来过夜。他们那儿乱哄哄，有的军官在大炮四周忙碌，有的军官会合在教堂围墙附近的广场上听设营官讲话，这时候忽然从教堂后边闪出一个穿便服的男子，骑着一匹奇怪的马。那匹浅黄色的小马生着好看的脖子和短短的尾巴，一步步走过来，然而不是照直走，却像是斜着溜过来，踩着一种细碎的舞步，仿佛有人用鞭子抽它的腿似的。骑马的人走到军官们面前，抬了抬帽子说：

“本地的地主，陆军中将冯·拉别克大人请诸位军官先生马上赏光到家里去喝茶……”

马低下头，踩着舞步，斜着身子往后退去。骑马的人又抬了抬帽子，一刹那间，跟他那匹奇怪的马隐到教堂后面，不见了。

“鬼才知道这是怎么回事！”有几个军官嘟哝道，他们正在散开，要回到自己的住处去，“大家都想睡觉了，这位冯·拉别克却要请人喝什么茶！什么叫作喝茶，我们心里可有数！”

所有六个连的军官们都清楚地记得去年的一件事：在阅兵期间，他们跟一个哥萨克团的军官们，也像这样受到一位伯爵地主——一位退伍军人的邀请去喝茶。那位好客、殷勤的伯爵款待他们，请他们吃饱、喝足之后，不肯放他们回到村里的住处去，却把他们留在自己家里过夜。所有这些当然都很好，简直没法儿希望更好的了，然而糟糕的是那位退伍军人有这些年轻人做伴，高兴得过了头。他对军官们讲他过去的光辉事迹，领他们走遍各处房间，给他们看名贵的画片、古老的版画、珍奇的武器，给他们念大人物的亲笔信，一直忙到太阳东升。那些疲乏厌倦的军官看着，听着，一心想睡觉，小心地对着袖口打呵欠。临了，主人总算放他们走了，可是要睡觉已经太迟了。

也许这个冯·拉别克就是这种人吧？是也好，不是也好，反正也没办法了。军官们换上整齐的军服，把周身收拾干净，成群结伙地去找那个地主的家。在教堂附近的广场上，他们打听出来要到那位先生的家可以沿着下面的路走——从教堂后面下坡到河边，沿着河岸走到一个花园，顺一条林荫路走到那所房子；或者走上面的路也成——从教堂照直顺着大路走，在离村子不到半俄里[1]的地方就到了地主的谷仓。军官们决定走上面的路。

“这个冯·拉别克是什么人？”他们一面走一面闲谈，“就是从前在普列夫纳统率 H 骑兵师的将领吧？”

“不，那人不叫冯·拉别克，单叫拉别克，没有冯。”

“多好的天气啊！”

大路在第一个谷仓那儿分成两股：一股照直往前去，消失在晦暗的暮色里；另一股往右去，通到主人的房子。军官们往右拐弯，讲话声音开始放低……路的两边排列着红房顶的石砌谷仓，笨重而森严，很像县城里的营房。前面，主人宅子的窗子里灯光明亮。

“好兆头，诸位先生！”有一个军官说，“我们的猎狗跑到大家前头去了。这是说，他闻出我们前头有猎物

1. 一俄里等于 1.06 千米。（说明：书中脚注除特别标明的之外，均为编者注。）

了！……”

中尉洛贝特科走在众人前面，他生得又高又结实，可是没长唇髭（他已经过二十五岁了，可是不知什么缘故，他那保养得很好的圆脸上却连一根胡子也没有），善于远远地辨出前面有女人，因此在这个旅里以这种嗅觉出名。他扭转身来说：

“对了，这儿一定有女人。我凭本能就觉出来了。”

冯·拉别克本人在正屋门口迎接军官们，他是一位仪表优雅、年纪大约六十岁的老人，穿着便服。他跟客人们握手，说他见到他们很高兴，很幸福，可是诚恳地请求军官先生们看在上帝的分上原谅他不留他们过夜。有两个带着孩子一起来的姐妹、几个弟兄、几个邻居来看望他，弄得他一个空房间也没有了。

将军跟每个人握手、道歉、微笑，可是凭他的脸色看得出他绝不像去年那位伯爵那么高兴接待这些客人，他之所以邀请这些军官，只是因为他觉得这是一种必要的礼节罢了。军官们自己呢，走上铺着柔软的毡毯的楼梯，一面听他讲话，一面觉得他们之所以受到邀请，也只是因为他不好意思不请他们罢了。他们看见听差们匆匆忙忙点亮楼下门道里和楼上前厅里的灯，觉得他们好像随

身把不安和不便带进了这个宅子。既然已经有两个带着子女的姐妹、弟兄、邻人大概由于家庭的喜事或者变故而聚会在这所房子里，那么十九个素不相识的军官的光临会受到欢迎吗？

到了楼上，在大厅门口，军官们遇到一位身材高大、匀称的老太太，长脸上生着黑眉毛，很像厄热尼皇后[1]。她殷勤而庄严地微笑着，说她看到客人很高兴，很幸福，道歉说她丈夫和她这回不能够邀请军官先生们在这里过夜。每逢她从客人面前扭转身去办点什么事，她那美丽、庄严的笑容立刻就消失了。那么，事情很清楚：她这一辈子见过很多军官，现在她对他们不感兴趣，即使她邀他们到家里来，而且表示歉意，那也只是因为她的教养和社会地位要求她这样做罢了。

军官们走进一个大饭厅，那儿已经有十来个人，男男女女，老老少少，坐在长桌的一边喝茶。在他们的椅子背后可以隐约看见一群男人笼罩在雪茄烟的轻飘的云雾里，他们当中站着一个瘦长的青年，正在谈论什么，他留着红色的络腮胡子，讲英国话，声音响亮，可是咬字不清。这群人的背后有一扇门，从门口望出去可以看

1. 厄热尼皇后（1826—1920），拿破仑三世的妻子。

见一个明亮的房间，摆着淡蓝色的家具。

“诸位先生，你们人数这么多，简直没法儿跟你们介绍了！”将军大声说，极力说得很快活，“自己介绍吧。诸位先生，不要客气！”

军官们有的带着很严肃的，甚至很严厉的脸相，有的现出勉强的笑容，大家都觉得很别扭，就好歹鞠一个躬，坐下来喝茶。

其中觉得最别扭的是里亚博维奇上尉。他是一个戴眼镜的军官，身材矮小，背有点伛偻，生着山猫样的络腮胡子。他的同伴们有的做出严肃的神情，有的露出勉强的笑容，他那山猫样的络腮胡子和眼镜却好像在说：“我是全旅当中顶腼腆、顶谦卑、顶没光彩的军官！”起初他刚走进饭厅以及后来坐下喝茶的时候，无论如何也不能够把注意力集中在一张脸或者一个东西上。那些脸、衣服、盛着白兰地的玻璃长颈酒瓶、杯子里冒出来的热气、有着雕塑装饰的檐板，这一切合成一个总的强大印象，在里亚博维奇心里引起不安，使他一心想把脑袋藏起来。他像第一回当众表演的朗诵者一样，虽然瞧见他眼前的一切东西，可是对看到的东西却不十分理解，按照生理学家的说法，这种虽然看见然而不理解的情况叫作“意

盲”。过了一会儿，里亚博维奇渐渐习惯新环境，眼睛亮了，就开始观察。他既是一个不善于交际的、腼腆的人，那么首先引起他注意的就是他自己最不行的，也就是他那些新相识的特别大胆的人。冯·拉别克，他的妻子，两位上了岁数的太太，一位穿淡紫色连衣裙的小姐，一个留着红色络腮胡子的青年（冯·拉别克的小儿子），仿佛事先排演过似的，很灵敏地夹在军官们当中坐好，立刻热烈地争论起来，弄得客人不得不插嘴。那位穿淡紫色衣服的小姐热烈地证明，做炮兵比做骑兵或者步兵轻松得多，冯·拉别克和上了岁数的太太们的看法则相反。紧跟着，大家七嘴八舌地谈起来。里亚博维奇瞧着淡紫色小姐十分激烈地争辩她所不熟悉的完全不感兴趣的事情，冷眼看出她脸上时而现出不诚恳的笑容，时而把笑容又收敛起来。

冯·拉别克和他的家人巧妙地把军官们引进争论中来，同时一刻也不放松地盯紧他们的杯子和嘴，注意他们是不是都在喝茶，是不是茶里都放了糖，为什么有人不吃饼干或者不喝白兰地。里亚博维奇看得越久，听得越久，他就越喜欢这个不诚恳的可是受过很好训练的家庭。

喝完茶以后，军官们走进客厅。洛贝特科中尉的本

能没有欺骗他，客厅里果然有许多小姐和年轻女人。“猎狗”中尉不久就站在一个穿黑色连衣裙、年纪很轻的金发女郎身旁，神气十足地弯下腰来，仿佛倚着一把肉眼看不见的军刀似的，微微笑着，风流地耸动肩膀。他大概在讲些很有趣味的荒唐话，因为金发女郎带着鄙夷的神情瞧着他那保养得很好的脸，淡漠地问一句：“真的吗？”猎狗倘若乖巧一点，从这不关痛痒的“真的吗”，应该可以推断出她未必喜欢这样的猎狗。

钢琴响了，忧郁的华尔兹舞曲从大厅里飘出敞开的窗口，不知什么缘故大家都想起来窗外现在是春天，五月的黄昏，人人都觉出空中有玫瑰、紫丁香、白杨的嫩叶的香气。在音乐的影响下，里亚博维奇喝下的那点白兰地正在起作用。他斜眼看着窗口，微微地笑，开始注意女人们的动作。他觉得玫瑰、白杨、紫丁香的气息好像不是从花园里飘来，而是从女人的脸上和衣服上冒出来的。

冯·拉别克的儿子请一位瘦弱的姑娘跳舞，跟她跳了两圈。洛贝特科在镶木地板上滑过去，飞到淡紫色小姐面前，带着她在大厅里翩翩起舞。跳舞开始了……里亚博维奇站在门旁，夹在不跳舞的人们当中，旁观着。

他这一辈子从没跳过一回舞，他的胳臂也从没搂过一回上流女人的腰。一个男人当着大家的面搂着一个不认得的姑娘的腰，让那姑娘把手放在自己的肩头，里亚博维奇看了总是很喜欢，可是他无论如何也不能想象自己会成为那样的男人。有些时候他嫉妒同伴们胆大、灵巧，心里很难过。他一想到自己胆小、背有点伛偻，没有光彩，腰细长，络腮胡子像山猫，就深深地痛心。可是年深日久，他也就习惯了，现在他瞧着同伴们跳舞，大声说话，不再嫉妒，光是觉得感伤罢了。

等到卡德里尔舞开始，小冯·拉别克就走到没跳舞的人们跟前，请两位军官去打台球。军官们答应了，跟他一块儿走出客厅。里亚博维奇没事可做，想参加大家的活动，就慢腾腾地跟着他们走去。他们从大厅里出来，走进客厅，然后走过一个有着玻璃顶棚的窄过道，走进一个房间。他们一进去，就有三个带着睡意的听差从沙发上很快地跳起来。小冯·拉别克和军官们穿过一长串房间，末后走进一个不大的房间，那里有一张台球桌子。他们就开始打台球。

里亚博维奇除了打纸牌以外从没玩过别的东西，他站在台球桌旁边，冷淡地瞧着打台球的人。他们呢，解

开上衣扣子，手里拿着球杆走来走去，说俏皮话，不断地嚷出一些叫人听不懂的词。打台球的人没注意他，只是偶尔有谁的胳臂肘碰着他，或者一不小心，球杆的一头戳着他，才扭转身来说一声：“对不起！”第一局还没打完，他就厌倦了，开始觉得他待在这儿是多余的，而且碍人家的事了……他想回到大厅里，就走出去了。

在回去的路上，他遇到一桩小小的奇事。他走到半路上，发现自己走错了地方。他清楚地记得在路上应当遇见三个带睡意的听差，可是他穿过五六个房间，那几个带着睡意的人好像钻到地底下去了。他发觉自己走错了，就扭转身退回一小段路，往右转弯，走进了他到台球房间去的时候没见过的一个昏暗的房间。他在那儿站了一会儿，犹豫不决地打开一扇他的眼睛偶然看见的门，走进一个漆黑的房间。他看见前面，正对面有一道门缝，从那道缝里射进一束明亮的光。门外面传来隐隐约约的、忧郁的玛祖卡舞曲的声音。这儿也跟大厅里一样，窗子敞开，有白杨、紫丁香和玫瑰的气味……

里亚博维奇迟疑地站住……这当儿，他出乎意料地听见匆匆的脚步声、连衣裙的沙沙声、喘吁吁的女人低语声：“到底来了！”有两条柔软的、香喷喷的、准定是

女人的胳膊搂住他的脖子，温暖的脸颊贴到他的脸颊上来，同时发出了亲吻的声音。可是那个亲吻的人立刻轻轻地惊叫了一声，抽身躲开他，而且里亚博维奇觉得她是带着憎恶躲开的。他也差点儿叫起来，就向门边的亮光跑过去……

他回到大厅里，心怦怦地跳，手抖得厉害，他连忙把手藏到背后去。起初他羞得不得了，生怕满大厅的人知道他刚刚被一个女人搂抱过、吻过。他畏畏缩缩，不安地往四下里看，可是等到他相信大厅里的人们跟先前一样平静地跳舞、闲谈，他就完全让一种生平从没经历过的新感觉抓住了。他起了一种古怪的变化……他的脖子刚才给柔软芳香的胳膊搂过，觉得好像抹了一层油似的。他左脸上靠近唇髭、经那个素不相识的人吻过的地方，有一种舒服的、凉酥酥的感觉，仿佛擦了一点薄荷水似的。他越是擦那地方，凉酥酥的感觉就越是厉害。他周身上下，从头到脚充满一种古怪的新感觉，那感觉越来越强烈……他情不自禁地想跳舞、谈话、跑进花园、大声地笑……他完全忘了他的背有点伛偻，他没有光彩，他有山猫样的络腮胡子，而且“貌不惊人”（这是有一回他偶然听到几个女人在谈到他的相貌时所用的形容词）。正巧冯·拉

别克的妻子走过他面前，他就对她亲切而欢畅地笑一笑，笑得她站住了，探问地瞧着他。

“我非常喜欢您这所房子！……”他说，正了一下眼镜。

将军的妻子微笑着，说这房子原是她父亲的。后来她问起他的父母是否还在世，他在军队里待得是不是很久，为什么他这么瘦……她的问题得到答复后，她便往前走去。他跟她谈过话以后，他的笑容比先前越发亲切，他觉得他的四周尽是些好人……

进晚餐的时候，里亚博维奇漫不经心地吃完给他端来的所有菜，自管喝酒，什么话也没听进去，极力要弄明白他方才遇到的究竟是怎么一回事。这件奇事具有神秘的、浪漫的性质，可是要解释却也不难。一定是有个姑娘或者太太跟别人约定在那个黑房间里相会。她等了很久，又烦躁又兴奋，竟把里亚博维奇当作她的情人了，尤其因为里亚博维奇走过那个黑房间的时候迟迟疑疑地站住，仿佛也在等什么人似的，那么这就更近情理了……里亚博维奇就照这样解释他何以会受到那样的一吻。

“不过她是谁呢？”他瞧了瞧四周女人的脸想道，“她一定年轻，因为老太太是不会去幽会的。而且她是个受

过教育的女人，这只要凭她衣服的沙沙声、她的香气、她的声调，就可以揣摩出来……”

他的目光停在淡紫色小姐的身上，他很喜欢她。她有美丽的肩膀和胳膊、聪明的脸、好听的声音。里亚博维奇瞧着她，希望那个不相识的女人就是她，而不是别人……可是她笑起来不怎么真诚，而且皱起她的长鼻子，这就使他觉得她显老了。然后他掉过眼睛去瞧那个穿黑色连衣裙的金发女郎。她年轻些，朴素些，真诚些，两鬓秀气，端起酒杯喝酒的样子很潇洒。现在里亚博维奇希望那个女人是她了。可是不久他又觉得她的脸平平常常，就掉过眼睛去瞧他身旁的那个女人……

“这是很难猜的，”他暗想，沉思着，“如若只要淡紫色小姐的肩膀和胳膊，再配上金发女郎的两鬓和洛贝特科左边坐着的那位姑娘的眼睛，那么……”

他暗自把这些东西搭配起来，就此凑成了吻过他的那个姑娘的模样。他希望她有那样的模样，可是在饭桌上又找不到。

晚餐以后，军官们酒足饭饱，精神抖擞，开始告辞和道谢。冯·拉别克和他的妻子又开始道歉，说是可惜不能留他们过夜。

“诸位先生，跟你们见面很高兴，很高兴！”将军说，这一回倒是诚恳的（大概因为人们在送走客人的时候总比在迎接客人的时候诚恳得多，也和蔼得多），“很高兴！希望你们回来路过的时候再光临！别客气！你们怎样走？你们要走上面的路吗？不，穿过花园走吧，下面那条路要近一点。”

军官们走出去，到了花园里。从充满亮光和喧闹声的地方走出来，花园里显得十分黑暗而宁静。他们沉默地一路走到花园门口。他们都有点醉意，兴致很好，心满意足，可是黑暗和静寂使他们沉思了一会儿。大概他们每个人都有着一种跟里亚博维奇相同的感触：将来是不是有一天他们也会像冯·拉别克一样有一所大房子、一个家庭、一个花园，即使本心并不诚恳，也能欢迎人们来，请他们吃得酒醉饭饱，使他们心满意足呢？

他们一走出花园门外，就开始争着讲话，无缘无故地大笑。他们现在顺小路走着，那条小路通到下面河边，然后沿着河岸向前伸展，绕过岸上的矮树丛、沟渠、枝条垂在水面上的柳树。河岸和小路都看不大清，对岸完全沉没在一片漆黑中。黑色的水面上这儿那儿映着星星，它们颤抖着，破碎了，只凭这一点才能推断河水流得很急。

空中没有一丝风。河对岸有些带着睡意的麻鹬在悲凉地鸣叫，在这边岸上一个矮树丛里有一只夜莺一点也不理会这群军官，仍然在放声歌唱。军官们在矮树丛四周站了一会儿，拿手指头碰一碰它，可是夜莺仍旧唱下去。

“这家伙可真了不得！”他们赞许地叫道，“我们站在它旁边，它却一点也不在乎！好一个坏蛋！”

在道路的尽头，小路爬上坡去，在教堂的围墙附近跟大路会合了。军官们爬上坡，累了，就在这儿坐下，点上纸烟。河对面现出一块暗红色的光亮。他们反正没事可做，就花了不少工夫推断那是野火呢，还是窗子里的灯亮，还是别的什么东西……里亚博维奇也瞧那亮光，他觉得那一块光在向他微笑，映眼，仿佛它知道那一吻似的。

里亚博维奇回到驻营地，赶快脱掉衣服，上了床。洛贝特科和美尔兹里亚科夫中尉（一个和气而沉静的人，在他那伙人中被看作很有学问的军官，他一有空就老是看《欧洲通报》，这份杂志他随便到哪儿去都随身带着）跟里亚博维奇住在同一所农民的小木房里。洛贝特科脱了衣服，带着还没玩畅的神情在房间里走来走去，走了很久，随后打发勤务兵去买啤酒。美尔兹里亚科夫上了床，

在枕头旁边放一支蜡烛，专心看那份《欧洲通报》。

“她是谁呢？”里亚博维奇瞧着被烟熏黑的天花板暗想。

他的脖子仍旧好像涂了油似的，嘴角旁边也仍旧带点凉意，仿佛擦了薄荷水一样。淡紫色小姐的肩膀和胳臂，穿黑衣服的金发女郎的两鬓和诚恳的眼睛、柳腰、衣服、胸针，在他的想象中闪动着。他极力注意这些形象，可是它们跳动着，逐渐变得模糊起来，摇曳不定。等到这些影子在每个人一闭上眼睛就会看见的宽阔的黑色背景上完全消失，他就开始听到匆忙的脚步声、衣裾的沙沙声、亲吻的响声，一种没来由的、强烈的欢乐就涌上他的心头……他正在尽情享受这种欢乐，却听见勤务兵回来报告，说是没有啤酒。洛贝特科气得要命，又开始走来走去。

“嘿，是不是蠢货？”他不断地说，先是在里亚博维奇面前站住，后来又在美尔兹里亚科夫面前站住，“连啤酒都买不着，真是个十足的蠢货，笨蛋！对不对？嘿，恐怕是个坏蛋吧？”

“在这一带当然买不到啤酒。”美尔兹里亚科夫说，眼睛却没离开《欧洲通报》。

“哦？您是这样看的吗？”洛贝特科坚持自己的意见，

“主啊，我的上帝，哪怕你把我送到月亮上去，我也会马上给您找着啤酒和女人！好，我马上就去找来……要是我找不着，您骂我是混蛋好了！”

他用很久的工夫穿上衣服，蹬上大皮靴，然后默默地抽完烟，走出去了。

“拉别克，格拉别克，拉别克，”他嘴里念着，却在前堂里站住了，“我一个人不高兴去，真该死！您肯出去溜达吗？啊？”

他没听见答话，就走回来，慢腾腾地脱掉衣服，上了床。美尔兹里亚科夫叹口气，收起《欧洲通报》，吹熄蜡烛。

“哼！……”洛贝特科嘟哝着，在黑暗里点上一支烟。

里亚博维奇拉起被子来蒙上头，蜷起身子，极力想把幻想中那些飘浮不定的影子拼凑起来，合成一个完整的人，可是任凭怎么样也拼凑不成。他不久就睡着了，他的最后一个思想是：不知一个什么人，对他温存了一下，使他喜悦，一件不平常的、荒唐的，可是非常美好快乐的事来到了他的生活里。哪怕在睡乡里，这个思想也没离开过他。

等到他醒来，他脖子上涂油的感觉和唇边薄荷的凉

意都没有了，可是欢乐的波浪还是跟昨天一样在他的心中起伏。他痴迷地瞧着给初升的阳光镀上一层金的窗框，听着街上行人走动的声音。贴近窗子，有人在大声讲话。里亚博维奇的连长列别杰兹基刚刚赶到旅里来，由于不习惯低声讲话，正在大声地跟他的司务长讲话。

“还有什么事？”连长嚷道。

“昨天他们换马掌的时候，官长，他们钉伤了‘鸽子’的蹄子。医士给涂上黏土和醋。现在他们用缰绳牵着它在边上走。还有，官长，昨天工匠阿尔捷米耶夫喝醉了，中尉下命令把他拴在一个后备炮架的前车上。”

司务长还报告说，卡尔波夫忘了带来喇叭上用的新绳和支帐篷用的木桩，还提到各位军官昨天傍晚到冯·拉别克将军家里去做客。话正谈到半中腰，窗口出现了列别杰兹基的生着红头发的脑袋。他眯着近视的眼睛瞧着军官们带着睡意的脸，跟他们打招呼。

“没什么事吧？”他问。

“那匹备了鞍子的辕马戴上新套具，把脖子磨肿了。”洛贝特科打着呵欠回答道。

连长叹口气，沉吟一下，大声说：

“我还要到阿列克山德拉·叶甫格拉佛芙娜那儿去一

趟。我得去看看她。好，再见吧。到傍晚我会追上你们的。”

过了一刻钟，炮兵旅动身上路了。这个旅沿着大道走，经过地主粮仓的时候，里亚博维奇瞧了瞧右边的房子。所有的窗口都拉下着百叶窗。房子里的人分明都在睡觉。昨天吻过里亚博维奇的那个女人也在睡觉。他极力想象她睡熟的样子。卧室的敞开的窗子，伸进窗口的绿树枝，早晨的新鲜空气，白杨、紫丁香、玫瑰的幽香，一张床，一把椅子，昨天沙沙响、现在放在椅子上的连衣裙，小小的拖鞋，桌上的小表，所有这些，他暗自描摹着，清楚而逼真，可是偏偏那要紧的、关键的东西，她的脸庞和梦中甜蜜的微笑，却从他的幻想里滑出去，就跟水银从手指缝中间漏掉了一样。他骑着马走出半俄里远，回过头来看：黄色的教堂、房子、河、花园，都沉浸在阳光里；那条河很美，两岸绿油油的，水中映着蓝天，河面上这儿那儿闪着银色的阳光。里亚博维奇向梅斯捷奇金村最后看了一眼，心里觉得很难过，好像跟一个很接近、很亲密的东西拆开了似的。

他眼前的路上，只有那些早已熟悉的、没有趣味的画面……左右两旁是未成熟的黑麦和荞麦的田野，有些乌鸦在田野上蹦来蹦去。往前看，只瞧见灰尘和人的后

脑勺儿。往后看，也只瞧见灰尘和人脸……打头的是四个举着佩刀步行前进的人，他们是前卫。后面，紧挨着的是一群歌手，歌手后面是骑马的司号员。前卫和歌咏队，像送葬行列中擎火炬的人一样，常常忘记保持规定的距离，远远地赶到前头去了……里亚博维奇随着第五连的第一门炮走着。他可以看见在他前面走动的所有四个连。在不是军人的人们看来，这个在行进的炮兵旅所形成的那条笨重的长行列好像是个复杂的、叫人不能理解的、杂乱无章的东西，谁也不明白为什么有那么多人围着一尊大炮，为什么那尊炮由那么多套着古怪的挽具的马拉着，仿佛那尊炮真是很可怕、很沉重似的。在里亚博维奇看来，这一切却十分清楚，因此一点也引不起他的兴趣。他老早就知道为什么每个连的前头除了军官以外还要有一个身材魁梧的士官骑在马上，为什么他叫作前导。紧跟在士官背后的是拉前套的马的骑手，随后是走在中间的马的骑手。里亚博维奇知道他们所骑的马，在左边的叫鞍马，在右边的叫副马，这些都很乏味。在那些骑手后面跟着两匹辕马。其中一匹马上坐着一个骑手，背上布满昨天的尘土，右腿上绑着一块粗笨的、样子可笑的小木头。里亚博维奇知道这块木头做什么用，并不觉得

可笑。所有的骑手随便地摇动短皮鞭，不时嚷一声。炮本身也不好看。前车上面堆了一袋袋的燕麦，盖着帆布。炮身上挂着茶壶、兵士的行囊、口袋，看上去那尊炮像是一头小小的、不伤人的动物，不知什么缘故被人们和马匹包围着。炮的两旁，有六个兵，都是炮手，背着风走路，挥动着胳膊。在这尊炮后面又是另外的前导、骑手、辕马，这后面又来了一尊炮，跟前面那尊同样难看，不威严。这第二尊炮过去以后，随后来了第三尊、第四尊，靠近第四尊炮有一个军官，等等。这个旅一共有六个连，每个连有四尊炮。这行列有半俄里长，殿后的是一串货车，货车旁边有一头极可爱的牲口，驴子玛加尔，那是一个连长从土耳其带来的，它耷拉着耳朵挺长的脑袋，沉思着迈着步子。

里亚博维奇冷淡地瞧瞧前面和后面，瞧瞧人的后脑勺儿和脸。换了别的时候，他大概已经迷迷糊糊，要睡着了，可是现在他却完全沉浸在愉快的新体验到的思绪中了。起初在炮兵旅刚刚启程的时候，他想说服自己：那件亲吻的事，如果有趣味，也只因为那是一个小小的、神秘的奇遇罢了，其实那是没什么意思的，把这件事看得认真，至少也是愚蠢的。可是不久他就顾不得这些道理，

想入非非了……他一会儿想着自己在冯·拉别克的客厅里，挨着一个姑娘，长得挺像淡紫色小姐和穿黑衣服的金发女郎；一会儿闭上眼睛，看见自己跟另一个完全不认得的姑娘待在一起，那人的脸相很模糊。他暗自跟她谈话，跟她温存，低下头去凑近她的肩头。他想象战争和离别，然后重逢，跟妻子儿女一块儿吃晚饭……

“煞住车！”每回他们下山，这个命令就响起来。

他也嚷着：“煞住车！”可是又生怕这一声喊搅乱他的幻梦，把他带回现实里来……

他们走过一个地主的庄园，里亚博维奇就隔着篱墙向花园里望。他的眼睛遇到一条很长的林荫路，像尺那么直，铺着黄沙土，夹道是新长出来的小桦树……他带着沉浸在幻想里的人的那份热情暗自想着女人的小小的脚在黄沙土上走着，于是突然间，在他的幻想中清清楚楚地出现了吻过他的那个姑娘的模样，正是昨天吃晚饭时候他描摹的那个样子。这个模样就此留在他的脑子里，再也不离开他了。

中午，后面靠近那串货车的地方有人嚷道：

“立正！向左看！军官先生们！”

旅长是一位将军，坐着一辆由一对白马拉着的马车

走过来了。他在第二连附近停住，嚷了一些谁也听不懂的话。好几个军官，里亚博维奇也在内，策动马，跑到他面前去。

“啊？怎么样？什么？”将军问，眏着他的红眼睛，“有病号吗？”

将军是个瘦小的男子，听到回答，就动着嘴，好像在咀嚼什么。他沉吟一下，对一个军官说：

“你们第三尊炮的炮车辕马的骑手摘掉了护膝，把它挂在炮的前车上了，那混蛋。您得惩罚他。”

他抬起眼睛看看里亚博维奇，接着说：

“我觉得你们那根车带太长了……”

将军又说了几句别的乏味的话，瞧着洛贝特科，微微地笑了。

“今天您看起来很忧愁，洛贝特科中尉，”他说，“您在想念洛普霍娃吧？对不对？诸位先生，他在想念洛普霍娃！”

洛普霍娃是个很胖很高的女人，年纪早已过四十了。将军自己喜欢身材高大的女人，年纪大小倒不论，因此猜想他手下的军官们也有同样的爱好。军官们恭敬地赔着笑脸。将军觉得自己说了句很逗笑很尖刻的话，心里

痛快，就扬声大笑，碰了碰他的车夫的后背，行了个军礼。马车往前驶走了……

“我现在所梦想的一切，我现在觉得不能实现的、人们少有的一切，其实是很平常的，”里亚博维奇瞧着将军车子后面的滚滚尘土，暗自想着，“这种事平常得很，人人都经历过……比方说，那位将军当初就谈过恋爱，现在结了婚，有了子女。瓦赫捷尔大尉，虽然后脑勺儿很红很丑，没有腰身，可也结了婚，有人爱……萨尔玛诺夫呢，很粗野，简直跟鞑靼人一样，可是他也谈过恋爱，最后结了婚……我跟大家一样，我早晚也会经历大家经历过的事……”

他想到自己是个平常的人，他的生活也平平常常，不由得很高兴，而且这给了他勇气。他由着性儿大胆描摹她和他自己的幸福，什么东西也不能束缚他的幻想了……

傍晚炮兵旅到达了驻扎地，军官们在帐篷里安歇，里亚博维奇、美尔兹里亚科夫、洛贝特科围着一口箱子坐着吃晚饭。美尔兹里亚科夫不慌不忙地吃着，他一面从容地咀嚼，一面看一本摆在他膝头上的《欧洲通报》。洛贝特科讲个没完，不断地往自己的杯子里斟啤酒。里亚博维奇做了一天的梦，脑筋都乱了，只顾喝酒，什么

话也没说。喝过三杯酒，他有点醉了，浑身觉着软绵绵的，就起了一种熬不住的欲望，想把他的新感觉讲给他的同事们听。

“在冯·拉别克家里，我遇到一件怪事……”他开口说，极力在自己的声调里加进满不在乎的、讥诮的口吻，“你们知道，我走进了台球房……”

他开始详详细细地述说那件亲吻的事，过了一会儿就沉默了……一会儿的工夫他已经把前后情形都讲完了，这件事只要那么短短的工夫就讲完，他不由得大吃一惊。他本来以为会把这个亲吻的故事一直讲到第二天早晨呢。洛贝特科是个爱说谎的人，因此什么人的话也不相信。他听里亚博维奇讲完，怀疑地瞧着他，冷冷地一笑。美尔兹里亚科夫动了动眉毛，眼睛没离开《欧洲通报》，说：

“上帝才知道这是怎么回事！……这女人一下子就搂住一个男人的脖子，也没叫一声他的名字……她一定是个心理变态的女人。”

“对了，一定是个心理变态的女人……”里亚博维奇同意。

“有一次我也遇见过这一类的事……”洛贝特科说，装出惊骇的眼神，“去年我上科甫诺去……我买了一张二

等客车的票……火车上挤得很，没法儿睡觉。我塞给乘务员半个卢布……他就拿着我的行李，领我到一个单人车室去……我躺下来，盖上毯子……你们知道，那儿挺黑。忽然我觉得有人碰了碰我的肩膀，朝我的脸上吹气。我动一动手，却碰到了不知什么人的胳膊肘。我睁开眼，你们猜怎么着，原来是一个女人！眼睛黑黑的，嘴唇红得好似一条新鲜的鲑鱼，鼻孔热情地呼气，胸脯活像一个软靠枕……”

“对不起，”美尔兹里亚科夫平静地插嘴，“关于胸脯的话，我倒能懂，可是既然那儿挺黑，你怎么看得清嘴唇呢？”

洛贝特科极力圆他的谎，嘲笑美尔兹里亚科夫缺乏想象力。这惹得里亚博维奇讨厌。他离开那口箱子，上了床，赌咒再也不向别人谈起这件事了。

露营生活开始了……日子一天天流过去，这一天跟那一天简直差不多。在那些日子，里亚博维奇的感情、思想、举动都像是在谈恋爱。每天早晨他的勤务兵给他送水来洗脸，他用冷水冲头的时候，总想起他的生活里有了一件美好而温暖的事。

到傍晚，他的同事们一谈到爱情和女人，他就走近

一点听着，脸上现出一种表情，仿佛兵士在听人述说他参加过的一个战役似的。有些天的傍晚，带着几分醉意的尉官们由“猎狗”洛贝特科领头到“城郊”去冶游，每逢里亚博维奇参加这类游乐的时候，他总是很难过，觉得深深的惭愧，暗自求“她”原谅……遇到空闲的当儿，或者失眠的夜晚，他回忆自己的童年、父亲、母亲，总之回想亲人的时候，他一定也会想起梅斯捷奇金村、那头怪马、冯·拉别克、他那长得像厄热尼皇后的妻子、那黑房间、门缝里漏进来的那一线亮光……

八月三十一日，他从露营地回去，然而不是跟整个炮兵旅，而是只跟其中的两个连一块儿走。他一路上梦想着，激动着，好像在回故乡似的。他热烈地盼望着再看见那匹怪马、那个教堂、冯·拉别克那个不诚恳的家庭、那黑房间。常常欺骗情人的那种“内心的声音”，不知什么缘故，向他悄悄说，他一定会看见她……他给种种疑问折磨着：他会怎样跟她见面？他跟她谈什么好呢？她忘了那回的亲吻没有？他想，就算事情真糟到这种地步，他竟不能再见到她，那么光是重走一遍那个黑房间，回想一下，在他也不失为一种乐趣……

将近傍晚，远远的地平线上出现了那熟悉的教堂和

白色的谷仓。里亚博维奇的心怦怦地跳起来……他没听见跟他并排骑着马的军官对他说了些什么，他把一切都丢在脑后，眼巴巴地瞧着在远处发亮的那条河，瞧着那所房子的房顶，瞧着鸽子窝，在夕阳的余晖中鸽子正在那上面飞来飞去。

他们走到教堂那儿，听设营官指定宿营地的时候，他时时刻刻巴望有一个骑马的人会从教堂的围墙后面走出来，请军官们去喝茶，可是……设营官讲完话，军官们下马，溜达到村里去了，那个骑马的人并没有来……

“冯·拉别克马上会从农民那儿听说我们来了，然后派人来请我们。”里亚博维奇想，这时候他走进农舍，不明白为什么一个同事点亮了一支蜡烛，为什么勤务兵忙着烧茶炊……

他心神不定。他躺下去，随后又起来，瞧着窗外，看那骑马的人来了没有。可是骑马的人没来。他就又躺下去，可是过了半个钟头他又起来，压不住心里的不安，就走到街上，向教堂走去。靠近教堂围墙的广场上又黑又荒凉……在下坡路那儿有三个兵士默默地排成一行，站在那儿。他们一看见里亚博维奇，就挺起腰板，行军礼。他回礼，开始顺着那条熟悉的小路走下去。

河对面，整个天空一片紫红色：月亮升上来了。有两个农妇大声说话，在菜园里摘白菜叶子。菜园后面有些小木房，颜色发黑……这边岸上的一切跟五月间一样：小路、矮树丛、挂在河面上的垂柳……不过那只勇敢的夜莺的声音却没有了，白杨和嫩草的香气也没有了。

里亚博维奇走到花园，往门里瞧，花园里黑暗而安静……他只看见近边桦树的白树干和一小段林荫路，别的东西全都化成漆黑的一团。里亚博维奇聚精会神地瞧着，听着，可是站了一刻钟工夫，既没听见一点声音，也没看见一点亮光，他就慢慢地往回走……

他走下坡，到了河边。将军的浴棚和挂在小桥栏杆上的浴巾，在他前面现出一片白色……他走到小桥上，站了一会儿，完全不必要地摸了摸浴巾，浴巾又粗又凉。他低下头看水……河水流得很快，在浴棚的木桩旁边发出勉强能听见的潺潺声。靠近左岸的河面上映着红月亮。小小的涟漪滚过月亮的倒影，把它拉长，扯碎，好像要把它带走似的……

“多么愚蠢，多么愚蠢啊！”里亚博维奇瞧着奔流的水，想着，“这是多么不近情理啊！”

现在他什么也不再盼望了，他这才清清楚楚地了解

了那件亲吻的事、他的焦躁、他的模糊的希望和失望。他想到他没有看见将军的使者，想到他永远也不会见到那个原该吻别人却错吻了他的姑娘，不再觉得奇怪了。刚好相反，要是他见到了她，那倒奇怪了……

河水奔流着，谁也不知道它流到哪儿去，为什么流。五月间它也像这样流，五月间它从小河流进大河，从大河流进海洋，然后化成蒸汽，变成雨水，也许如今在里亚博维奇面前流过去的仍旧是原先的那点水吧……这是为什么？为什么呢？

里亚博维奇觉得整个世界，整个生活，都好像是一个不能理解的、没有目的的玩笑……他从水面上移开眼睛，瞧着天空，又想起命运怎样化为一个不相识的女人对他偶然温存了一下，想起他的夏天的迷梦和幻象，他这才觉得他的生活异常空洞，贫乏，没有光彩……

他回到他住的农舍里，没有碰见一个同事。勤务兵报告说，他们都到“冯特利亚勃金将军”家里去了，因为将军派了一个骑马的使者来邀请他们……一刹那间里亚博维奇心里腾起一股欢乐，可是他立刻扑灭它，上了床。他存心跟他的命运作对，仿佛要惹它气恼似的，偏不到将军家去。

大沃洛嘉和小沃洛嘉

“放开我，我要自己赶车！我要坐到车夫旁边去！”索菲雅·利沃芙娜大声说，“车夫，你等一等，我要跟你一块儿坐在赶车座位上。”

她在雪橇上站着，她的丈夫符拉季米尔·尼基狄奇和她小时候的朋友符拉季米尔·米海雷奇抓住她的胳膊，免得她跌倒。那辆三套马的雪橇跑得飞快。

“我早就说不该给她喝白兰地，”符拉季米尔·尼基狄奇烦恼地小声对他的旅伴说，“你这个人啊，真是的！”

上校凭经验知道，像他的妻子索菲雅·利沃芙娜这样的女人在这种带点醉意的、疯疯癫癫的快乐过去以后，紧跟着照例就是歇斯底里的大笑，接着是痛哭。他担心

过一会儿他们回到家里以后，他没法儿睡觉，而不得不忙着张罗冷敷布和药水。

“嘘！”索菲雅·利沃芙娜叫道，“我要赶车。”

她心里真是快活和得意。自从举行婚礼那天起，最近两个月来，总有一个想法煎熬着她，她觉得她嫁给亚吉奇上校是因为贪图富贵，而且像人们常说的那样，因为赌气[1]；可是今天在城郊那家饭店里，她终于相信自己热烈地爱着他。尽管他已经五十四岁，却身材匀称，头脑机敏，动作灵活，擅长说俏皮话，给茨冈姑娘们伴唱。真的，如今老头倒比青年可爱一千倍，仿佛老人和青年掉换了位置似的。尽管上校比她父亲还要大两岁，而她只有二十三岁，然而凭良心说，论精力和朝气，他却比她不知超出多少，那么，年纪大又有什么关系呢？

“啊，我亲爱的！”她暗想，“了不起的人！”

在那家饭店里，她还相信，她那旧日的感情已经连影子也没有了。对她小时候的朋友符拉季米尔·米海雷奇，或者简称沃洛嘉，她昨天还爱得发疯，爱得要命，现在却完全淡漠了。今天整个傍晚，她觉得他无精打采，带着睡意，不招人喜欢，一无可取。他在饭店里照例厚着

1. 原文为法语。

脸皮避免付账，这一回他的这种态度使她暗暗生气，好容易才忍住没对他说：“要是您没钱，就该坐在家里才对。”每次都是由上校一个人付钱。

也许由于她眼前不断地闪过树木、电线杆和雪堆吧，总之，各式各样的思想涌上了她的心头。她想起饭店的账单是一百二十卢布，另外还付给茨冈人一百卢布。明天，只要她乐意，她可以随便挥霍上千的卢布，可是两个月以前，在她结婚以前，她自己连三个卢布都没有，随便买一点小东西都得向她父亲要钱。生活的变化是多么大呀！

她的思路千头万绪，她想起当初她十岁的时候，她现在的丈夫亚吉奇上校追求过她的姑母，全家人都说他把她害苦了，事实上，她姑母走出房来吃饭的时候确实常常脸上带着泪痕，而且老是坐上马车不知到什么地方去。大家讲起她来总是说：这个可怜的人休想得到安宁了。那时候他很漂亮，大受女人们的垂青。因此全城的人都知道他，大家说他似乎每天都要分头到那些爱慕他的女人的家里去一趟，就跟医生去给病人看病一样。现在呢，尽管他头发白了，脸上起了皱纹，戴了眼镜，可是他那张瘦脸，特别是从侧面看过去，有时候还是显得挺漂亮的。

索菲雅·利沃芙娜的父亲是个军医官，从前跟亚吉奇在同一个部队里共过事。沃洛嘉的父亲也是军医官，从前也跟亚吉奇上校和她父亲在同一个部队里共过事。沃洛嘉虽然常常闹出很复杂、很烦心的恋爱纠纷，可是学业优良，他在大学毕业的时候，成绩极好，现在选定外国文学作为他的专业，据说正在写论文。他住在他那做军医的父亲的营房里，虽然三十岁了，自己却没有钱。索菲雅·利沃芙娜小时候和他同住在一栋房子里，虽然两家各有自己的一套住宅。他常来找她一块儿游玩，一块儿学跳舞，一块儿学说法国话。可是等到他长大，变成一个身材匀称、十分漂亮的青年，她见着他就怕羞了，后来暗自发疯似的爱上他，直到最近嫁给亚吉奇为止。他也很受女人们的垂青，差不多从十四岁起，他就善于博得她们的欢心，那些为他而对丈夫不忠诚的太太，总是借口沃洛嘉年纪还小而为自己辩白。不久以前有人讲起他，说他做大学生的时候，住在大学附近的公寓房间里，每次有人去找他，敲他的房门，就会听见门里面响起他的脚步声，然后是低声的道歉："对不起，我不是一个人在屋里。"[1] 亚吉奇很欣赏他，夸奖他前途无量，就像杰尔

1. 原文为法语。

查文[1]对待普希金一样，显然，亚吉奇喜欢他。他们两人往往一连几个钟头沉默地打台球或者玩“辟开”[2]。亚吉奇如果坐上三套马的马车到什么地方去，总是把沃洛嘉带在身边，沃洛嘉也只把他论文的秘密讲给亚吉奇一个人听。当初上校比较年轻的时候，他们常常处于情敌的地位，可是彼此从来也不争风吃醋。在他们常常同去的社交场所，大家总是管亚吉奇叫作大沃洛嘉，管他的朋友叫作小沃洛嘉。

在雪橇上，除了大沃洛嘉、小沃洛嘉和索菲雅·利沃芙娜以外，还有一个女人，就是玛尔迦莉达·亚历山德罗芙娜，大家称呼她莉达。她是亚吉奇太太的表姐，一个三十岁开外的姑娘，脸色十分苍白，眉毛漆黑，戴着夹鼻眼镜，不停地吸纸烟，哪怕在天气严寒的时候也一样。她的胸前和膝盖上老是有烟灰。她说话带着鼻音，拖长每个字的字音，性情冷僻，随便喝多少蜜酒和白兰地总也不会醉，时常懒洋洋而又乏味地讲些含意暧昧的掌故。她在家里从早到晚翻看厚本的杂志，弄得杂志上

1. 杰尔查文（1743—1816），俄罗斯诗人。1815 年 1 月 8 日，年轻的普希金在皇村学校参加考试时，当众朗诵他的诗篇，受到杰尔查文的赞赏。

2. 一种纸牌游戏。

撒满烟灰，或者吃冰冻的苹果。

“索尼雅[1]，别发疯了，”她用唱歌般的声调说，“真的，这简直是愚蠢。”

在临近城门的地方，那三套马的雪橇跑得慢了点，房屋和行人不断闪过去。索菲雅·利沃芙娜平静下来，偎紧她的丈夫，专心想心事。小沃洛嘉坐在她对面。这时候，除了轻松快活的思想以外，又添上些阴郁的思想。她暗想，坐在对面的这个人知道她爱他，他当然相信她是因为赌气嫁给上校的说法。她一次也没有向他表白过爱情，而且不希望他知道，总是隐瞒着她自己的感情，可是从他的脸色看得出他十分了解她，这就伤了她的自尊心。不过在她的处境里最使她痛心的是，自从举行婚礼以后，这个小沃洛嘉倒忽然开始对她献起殷勤来，而这是以前从来也没有过的。他往往一连几个钟头默默地陪她坐着，或者谈些闲话，此刻在雪橇里他没有跟她谈话，却微微地踩着她的脚，握握她的手。显然，他一心巴望她出嫁。他分明看不起她，她就像那种不规矩的坏女人那样在他心里只能引起某种性质的兴趣。当那种得意的感情和对丈夫的爱情跟屈辱的感情和受伤的自尊心在她

1. 索尼雅和下文的索涅琪卡均为索菲雅的爱称。

心里混在一起的时候，她就不禁生出逞强的心，只想坐到赶车座位上去，嚷一阵，吹一阵口哨……

在他们的马车经过一个女修道院的当儿，院里那口一千普特[1]重的大钟敲响了。莉达在胸前画十字。

“我们的奥丽雅在这个修道院里。”索菲雅·利沃芙娜说，也在胸前画十字，身子哆嗦了一下。

“为什么她进了修道院？”上校问道。

“因为赌气，”莉达生气地回答说，显然暗指索菲雅·利沃芙娜和亚吉奇的婚姻，“现在这种因为赌气挺时行。它正向全世界挑战。她原是个爱说爱笑、极爱卖弄风情的女人，只喜欢舞会和舞伴，可是忽然间，她走了！弄得人人都吃了一惊！”

“这不是实情，”小沃洛嘉放下皮大衣的衣领，露出他那张漂亮的脸，说，“这跟赌气不相干，不瞒您说，这完全是由于遭了灾祸。她哥哥德米特利被流放去服苦役，如今下落不明。她母亲伤心而死。”

他又竖起他的衣领。

“奥丽雅做得好，”他声音低沉地接着说，“她处在养女的地位，况且又跟索菲雅·利沃芙娜那样的好人住在

1. 俄国重量单位。一普特等于 16.38 千克。

一起，这一点也得考虑到才是！”

索菲雅·利沃芙娜从他的声调里听出轻蔑的口气，就想说几句话顶撞他，可是她没说出口。她又生出那种逞强的心情。她站起来，带着哭腔叫道：

“我要去做晨祷！车夫，往回走！我要去见见奥丽雅！”

雪橇往回驶去。修道院的钟声低沉，索菲雅·利沃芙娜感到这声音使人联想到奥丽雅和她的生活。别的教堂也在敲钟。等到车夫勒住那三匹马，索菲雅·利沃芙娜就跳下雪橇，独自一个人，也不要人陪伴，很快地往大门走去。

“劳驾，快一点！”她丈夫对她叫道，“时候已经不早了！”

她走进乌黑的大门口，然后顺着一条从大门通到大教堂的林荫路走去，积雪在她脚底下吱吱地响，钟声就在她的上空轰鸣，仿佛使她的全身震颤。她来到教堂门口，走下三层台阶，然后穿过一道门廊，两旁都是圣徒的画像，弥漫着刺柏和神香的气味。随后又是一道门，有一个穿黑衣服的人给她开门，对她深深地鞠躬……教堂里，晨祷还没开始。有一个修女在圣像壁旁边走动，点燃高烛

台上的蜡烛，另一个修女点燃枝形烛台上的蜡烛。这儿那儿，圆柱附近和侧祭坛附近，有些黑色人影站着不动。“大概，他们现在这样站着，一直不离开，要到明天早晨才走吧。”索菲雅·利沃芙娜暗想。她觉得这儿又黑又冷，枯燥乏味，比墓园里还要乏味。她带着烦闷的感觉瞧着那些一动不动、呆若木鸡的人影，忽然她的心收紧了。不知怎的，她认出一个身量不高、肩膀窄小、头戴黑色三角头巾的修女就是奥丽雅，其实奥丽雅进修道院的时候长得挺胖，身量也似乎高一些。索菲雅·利沃芙娜不知什么缘故，心里十分激动，犹豫不决地走到那个见习修女跟前，从她肩膀上望过去，看清了她的脸，果然她就是奥丽雅。

“奥丽雅！”她说，举起两只手轻轻一拍，兴奋得说不出话来，“奥丽雅！”

那个修女立刻认出她来，惊讶地扬起眉毛。她那张刚洗过的、干净而苍白的脸高兴得放光，就连她那三角头巾下露出的白色包头布也似乎高兴得放光了。

“瞧，主赐的奇迹。”她说着，也举起她那两只干瘦的白手拍了一下。

索菲雅·利沃芙娜紧紧地抱住她，吻她，同时又担

心别冒出酒气来。

“刚才我们路过这儿，想起了你。”她说，喘不过气来，好像刚才很快地跑过一段路似的，“你的脸色多么苍白啊，上帝！我……我见着你高兴极了。哦，怎么样？怎么样？你觉得寂寞吗？”

索菲雅·利沃芙娜往四下里看一眼别的修女们，接着低声说：

“我们那儿发生了好多变化。……你知道，我嫁给亚吉奇，符拉季米尔·尼基狄奇了。你一定记得他。……我跟他在一块儿，很幸福。”

“好，感谢上帝。你父亲身体好吗？”

“好。他常想起你。你，奥丽雅，到了假日务必来看我们。听见了吗？”

“我会去的，”奥丽雅说，微微一笑，“我明天就去。”

索菲雅·利沃芙娜自己也不知道为什么，哭起来了。她不出声地哭了一会儿，然后擦干眼泪说：

“莉达没有见到你，会觉得十分惋惜。她跟我们一块儿出来的。沃洛嘉也在。他们就在大门口。要是你能跟他们见面，他们会多么高兴啊！我们去找他们吧，反正祈祷还没开始。”

“那我们就去吧。”奥丽雅同意说。

她在胸前画了三次十字，然后跟索菲雅·利沃芙娜一块儿往门口走去。

“那么，索涅琪卡，你说你挺幸福？”她走出大门的时候问道。

“很幸福。”

“好，感谢上帝。”

大沃洛嘉和小沃洛嘉看见这个修女走出来，就跳下雪橇，恭恭敬敬向她问好。他们看见她那苍白的脸和黑色的修女服显然都感动了。而且，她还记得他们，出来向他们问候，两人心里暗暗高兴。索菲雅·利沃芙娜怕她冻着，就拿过一条车毯披在她身上，同时用她皮大衣的一块前襟把她裹住。方才的眼泪使她的心头轻松了一些，灵魂变得纯净了。她暗自欣喜，这个热闹的、不安宁的、实际上不纯洁的夜晚竟然出人意料，这样纯洁而温柔地结束了。为了要奥丽雅在她身边多留一会儿，她提议说：

“让她坐上雪橇兜一阵吧！奥丽雅，你坐上去，我们一会儿就回来。”

两个男人预料修女会拒绝，圣徒是不坐三套马的雪

橇兜风的。可是使他们吃惊的是，她居然同意，还坐上了雪橇。这辆三套马的雪橇往城门那边跑去，大家都默不作声，只是极力让她坐得舒服点，暖和点，每个人都暗想她从前是什么样子，现在又是什么样子。现在她的脸缺乏热情，很少表情，冷淡而苍白，而且透明，好像她的血管里流着的是水而不是血。不过两三年前，她却长得丰满，脸颊绯红，常常谈论那些追求她的男人，为一丁点儿小事而扬声大笑。

在城门附近，雪橇掉转头往回跑，过了大约十分钟，在修道院门前停住，奥丽雅走下雪橇。钟楼上，钟声响得更急了。

“求主保佑你们。”奥丽雅说，照修女那样深深一鞠躬。

“那么你一定要来，奥丽雅。”

“我会去的，会去的。”

她很快地走了，不久就消失在乌黑的大门里。这以后，雪橇往回跑，不知什么缘故，大家心里都感到十分愁闷。人人都沉默不语。索菲雅 · 利沃芙娜觉得浑身发软，心情沮丧。她觉得刚才逼着修女坐上雪橇，夹在一伙喝过酒的人当中，乘着三套马的雪橇兜风，未免荒唐、鲁莽，而且几乎可以说是不敬。她的酒意过去了，欺骗自己的

愿望也就随之而消失，她已经清楚地感到她不爱她的丈夫，而且也不可能爱他，这件事简直是胡闹、愚蠢。她嫁给他是由于贪图富贵，因为他，按她中学里的女同学的说法，“阔绰得不得了”；又由于她生怕自己像莉达似的做老处女；还由于她厌烦她那做军医的父亲，而且想气气小沃洛嘉。要是她出嫁前能够预料到生活会这样沉重、可怕、讨厌，那么，就是拿全世界的财富都送给她，她也不会同意结婚。然而现在已经无法挽回。只好听天由命了。

他们回到家里。索菲雅·利沃芙娜在暖和而柔软的床上躺下，盖好被子，于是想起那道幽暗的门廊、那种神香的气味、那些圆柱旁边的人影。她想到在她睡着以后，那些人将会始终站着不动，就不由得害怕。晨祷的时间很长，然后是念经，然后是弥撒，祈祷……

“可是要知道，上帝是有的，一定是有的，而我总会死的，那就是说，我早晚得考虑灵魂，考虑永恒的生活，像奥丽雅一样。奥丽雅现在得救了，她给自己解决了所有的问题。……可是万一没有上帝呢？那她的一生就白白糟蹋了。可是怎么会是白白糟蹋呢？为什么就是白白糟蹋呢？”

过了一会儿又有些思想萦回在她的脑际：

“上帝是有的，死亡一定会来临，应当想到灵魂才对。如果奥丽雅此刻知道她马上会死掉，她也不会害怕。她准备好了。主要的是她已经为自己解决了人生的问题。上帝是有的……是啊……可是除了进修道院以外，难道就没有别的出路了？要知道，进修道院无非是放弃生活，毁掉生活罢了……”

索菲雅·利沃芙娜有点害怕。她把脑袋埋在枕头底下。

“不应当想这些，”她小声说，“不应当。”

亚吉奇在隔壁房间里的地毯上走来走去，他的马刺轻轻地响着，他在想心事。索菲雅·利沃芙娜猛地想到这个人只在一点上使她感到亲切和可爱：他的名字也叫符拉季米尔。她从床上坐起来，柔声叫道：

“沃洛嘉！”

“什么事？”她丈夫应声说。

“没什么。”

她又躺下去。钟声响起来，也许就是修道院里的钟声吧。她又不由得想起那道门廊和那些乌黑的人影。那些关于上帝和不可避免的死亡的想法在她头脑里盘旋，她就用被子蒙住头，免得听见钟声。她暗想，在衰老和

不可避免的死亡来临以前，还有很长很长一段生活要过，她得每天忍受这个她所不爱的、此刻走进寝室里来睡觉的男子的亲近，她得扑灭她心里对另一个年轻迷人而且在她看来不平凡的男子的无望的爱情。她看一眼丈夫，想对他道一声晚安，可是没有说出口，却忽然哭起来。她恼恨自己。

“得，音乐开始了！”亚吉奇说，把“乐”字说得很重。

她哭了很久，一直到早晨九点多钟才平静下来。她停了哭，全身不再发抖，可是头痛欲裂。亚吉奇匆匆地赶着去做晚弥撒，在隔壁房间里抱怨帮他穿衣服的勤务兵。他到卧室里来取东西，马刺发出轻微的响声，后来又进来一趟，这一回已经戴上带穗的肩章和勋章了。他两条腿由于害风湿病而有点瘸。不知什么缘故，索菲雅·利沃芙娜觉得他的模样和步法像一头猛兽。

她听见亚吉奇在打电话。

“费心，请您接瓦西里耶夫营房！”他说。过了一会儿他又说：“瓦西里耶夫营房吗？劳驾，请萨里莫维奇医生接电话……”又过了一会儿：“是哪一位啊？是你吗，沃洛嘉？很高兴。亲爱的，请你父亲马上到我们家里来一趟，因为我的妻子昨天回来以后，觉得很不舒服。你

是说他不在家？哦……谢谢。太好啦……非常感谢……谢谢[1]。”

亚吉奇第三次走进寝室来，弯下腰凑近他妻子，在她胸前画个十字，伸出手去让她吻（凡是爱他的女人都吻他的手，他已经养成习惯了），说他吃午饭的时候回来。他说完就走了。

十一点多钟，使女通报说，符拉季米尔·米海雷奇来了。索菲雅·利沃芙娜又疲乏又头痛，身子摇摇晃晃，很快地穿上她那件用毛皮镶边、又新又漂亮的淡紫色家常便服，赶紧把头发好歹梳理一下。她觉得她的灵魂里生出一种无法形容的温柔感情，高兴得周身发抖，生怕他会走掉。她只巴望看他一眼。

小沃洛嘉这次来访，装束整齐，穿着燕尾服，打着白领结。索菲雅·利沃芙娜走进客厅里，他吻她的手，为她身体不爽而真诚地表示难过。后来他们坐下来，他就称赞她那件便服。

“昨天跟奥丽雅见过面以后，我心里很乱，”她说，“起初我感到害怕，而现在却羡慕她了。她好比牢不可破的山岩，谁都休想搬得动它。可是，沃洛嘉，难道她就没

1. 原文为法语。

有别的出路了？难道活生生地埋葬自己才算是解决了人生问题？要知道，那是死而不是生啊。”

一提起奥丽雅，小沃洛嘉的脸上就现出感动的神情。

“您，沃洛嘉，是个聪明人，”索菲雅·利沃芙娜说，“请您指点我，好让我也能像她那样行事。当然，我不是个信徒，不会进修道院，不过我还是可以做些性质相似的事。我生活得不轻松啊。”她沉默一阵以后，接着说，“您指点我吧。……告诉我一种可以使我信服的办法。您哪怕只说一句话也好。”

“一句话？好吧：砰的一声响！”

“沃洛嘉，为什么您看不起我？”她痛心地问道，“您跟我讲起话来，原谅我这样说，总是用一种纨袴子弟的特别口气，不像是对朋友，对正派的女人讲话。您很有成就，您喜欢科学，可是为什么您从来也不对我谈科学呢？为什么？我不配吗？”

小沃洛嘉烦恼地皱起眉头，说：

“为什么您忽然需要起科学来了？也许您还需要宪法吧？或者需要鲟鱼肉烧辣根？”

“哦，好吧，我是个一无可取、渺小庸俗、品行不端、浅薄愚蠢的女人。……我干过许许多多错事，我心理变态，

道德败坏，我活该受到轻视。可是话得说回来，您，沃洛嘉，年纪比我大十岁，我的丈夫比我大三十岁。我是在你们眼前长大的，要是你们乐意，你们就可以随意把我培养成任什么样的人，哪怕培养成天使也未尝办不到。可是你们……”她的嗓音颤抖了，“这么可怕地对待我。亚吉奇年纪老了却跟我结婚，您呢……”

“哎，得了，得了，”沃洛嘉说，坐近一点，吻她的双手，“让叔本华去谈哲学，去证明他要证明的事吧，我们呢，还是来吻这两只小手的好。”

“您看不起我，但愿您能知道我为这种态度多么难过才好！”她迟疑地说，事先就知道他不会相信她的话。“但愿您知道我多么希望变个样子，开始过一种新的生活！我一想到这里就十分兴奋，”她说，果然兴奋得流下泪来，“我想做一个诚实纯洁的好人，不作假，有生活目标。”

“行了，行了，行了，劳驾，别装腔作势了！我不喜欢这样！”沃洛嘉说，脸上现出不痛快的神情，“说真的，这简直像是演戏了。我们还是做普通人的好。”

她怕他生气走掉，就赶紧辩白，而且做出勉强的笑容来向他讨好，又讲起奥丽雅，讲到她一心想解决她的人生问题，开始做一个堂堂正正的人。

“砰的……一声……响……”他低声唱起来，“砰的……一声……响……”

猛然间，他搂住她的腰。她自己也不知道自己在做什么，把两只手放在他的肩膀上，一时间痴迷地，仿佛在雾里似的，瞧着他那张聪明而讥诮的脸、额头、眼睛、漂亮的胡子……

“你自己早就知道我爱你，”她对他承认道，痛苦地红了脸，甚至感到她的嘴唇由于羞耻而抽搐起来，“我爱你。可是你为什么折磨我呢？”

她闭上眼睛，热烈地吻他的嘴唇，吻了大约有一分钟之久。虽然她知道这不正派，连他都会指责她，而且可能有使女走进来，不过她无论如何也没法儿结束这一吻。……

“啊，你在怎样折磨我呀！”她又说了一遍。

过了半个钟头，他得到他所需要的一切以后，在饭厅里坐下来吃东西。她跪在他面前，贪婪地瞧着他的脸。他就对她说，她活像一条小狗，等着人家丢给它一小块火腿吃。后来他叫她坐在他的膝头上，拿她当小娃娃似的摇来摇去，嘴里唱着：

“砰的……一声……响！”

临到他准备告辞，她就用热烈的口气问他：

“什么时候？今天吗？在什么地方？”

她伸出两只手凑到他的嘴边，好像要用手去抓住他的答话似的。

“今天恐怕不方便了，”他沉吟一下说，“明天也许行。”

他们就分手了。午饭前，索菲雅·利沃芙娜坐上雪橇到修道院里去找奥丽雅，可是到了那边，人家告诉她说奥丽雅外出为死人念赞美诗去了。她从修道院里出来，又坐上雪橇去找她父亲，也没在他家里碰到他，然后她就换一辆雪橇，毫无目的地串大街，走小巷，照这样坐车一直游逛到傍晚。不知什么缘故，她老是想起她那脸上带着泪痕、坐立不安的姑母。

到晚上，他们又坐上三套马的雪橇，到城郊饭店里去听茨冈人唱歌。当他们再次路过修道院的时候，索菲雅·利沃芙娜想起奥丽雅，不由得心惊肉跳，因为她思忖，对她这个圈子里的姑娘和女人来说，除了坐着三套马的车子不停地逛荡，说谎，或者索性进修道院去扑灭生机以外，就没有别的出路了……

第二天索菲雅·利沃芙娜去赴幽会，然后又孤身一人坐在街头的雪橇上跑遍全城，心里想着她的姑母。

过了一个星期，小沃洛嘉把她丢开了。这以后生活又照原样进行，仍旧那么没趣味，无聊，有时候甚至痛苦。上校和小沃洛嘉打了很久的台球和玩“辟开”，莉达懒洋洋地、乏味地讲那些掌故，索菲雅·利沃芙娜老是坐着街头的雪橇游逛，或者要求她丈夫带她坐着三套马的雪橇去兜风。

她几乎每天都到修道院去，惹得奥丽雅厌烦了。她对奥丽雅诉说自己难以忍受的痛苦，哭哭啼啼，同时又感到她一走进修道院，就随身带进一种不洁、可怜、陈腐的东西。奥丽雅呢，老是用背书的腔调不动感情地对她说：这些都没关系，一切都会过去，上帝会宽恕她的。

醋栗

从大清早起，整个天空就已经布满了雨云。那天没风，不热，可是闷。每逢晦暗的阴天，乌云挂在田野的上空，久久不散，看样子会下雨而又不下的时候，往往就会有这样的天气。兽医伊万·伊万内奇和中学教师布尔金已经走累了，依他们看来田野好像没有尽头似的。前面远处，隐约可以看见米罗诺西茨戈耶村的风车，右边有一排高岗，伸展出去，越过村子，消失在远方。他们俩都知道那是河岸，那儿有草场、绿油油的柳树、庄园，要是站在一个高岗的顶上望出去，就可以看见同样辽阔的田野和电报线，远处的一列火车，像是一条毛毛虫在爬，遇上晴朗的天气，从那儿甚至可以看得见城市。如今，在

没风的天气，整个大自然显得那么温和而沉静。伊万·伊万内奇和布尔金对这片田野生出满腔热爱，两人都心想：这个地方多么辽阔、多么美丽啊。

“上一次我们在村长普罗科菲的堆房里，”布尔金说，“您打算讲一个故事来着。”

“对了，当时我原想讲一讲我弟弟的事。”

伊万·伊万内奇深深地叹一口气，点上烟斗，预备开口讲故事，可是正巧这时候下雨了。过了大约五分钟，雨下大了，空中乌云密布，很难预测这场雨什么时候才会停。伊万·伊万内奇和布尔金站住，考虑起来。他们的狗已经淋湿，站在那儿，用后腿夹着尾巴，深情地瞧着他们。

“我们得找个地方避一避雨才好，”布尔金说，“那就到阿廖欣家去吧。离这儿挺近。”

“那我们就去吧。”

他们就往斜下里拐过去，穿过已经收割过的田地，时而照直走，时而往右拐，直到走上一条大道为止。不久就出现了杨树，园子，然后是谷仓的红房顶；有一条河，河水闪闪发光，顿时眼界豁然开朗，前面是一大片水，有一个磨坊和一个白色的浴棚。这就是阿廖欣所住的索

菲诺村。

磨坊在工作，声音盖过了雨声，水坝在颤抖。有几匹淋湿的马垂着头，站在大车旁边。人们披着麻袋走来走去。这儿潮湿、泥泞、憋闷，看上去河水冰凉，凶险。伊万·伊万内奇和布尔金已经觉得周身潮湿、不清爽、不舒服，脚沾着烂泥而变得挺重。他们穿过水坝，爬上坡，往地主的谷仓走去，一路上都没讲话，好像在互相生气似的。

有一个谷仓里筛谷机轰轰地响。仓门开着，滚滚的灰尘冒出来。阿廖欣本人就在门口站着，这是一个四十岁光景的男子，又高又胖，头发很长，与其说像地主，不如说像教授或者画家。他穿一件很久没有洗过的白衬衫，拦腰系一根绳子，算是腰带，下身没穿外裤，只穿了一条长衬裤，靴子上也沾满了泥浆和麦秸。他的眼睛和鼻子扑满灰尘，变得乌黑。他认出了伊万·伊万内奇和布尔金，显然很高兴。

“请到屋里去吧，两位先生，”他含笑说道，“我马上就来，用不了一分钟。”

这是一所两层楼的大房子。阿廖欣住在楼下两个带拱顶的房间里，窗子很小，从前原是管家们居住的。屋

里陈设简单，有黑面包、便宜的白酒和马具的气味。楼上的正房他难得去，只有客人来了他才去一趟。伊万·伊万内奇和布尔金在房子里遇到一个使女，是个年轻女人，长得那么美，他俩不由得同时站住，互相瞧了一眼。

“你们再也想不出我看见你们有多么高兴，两位先生，”阿廖欣说，跟着他们一块儿走进前厅，“这可是万万没想到！佩拉格娅，”他对那使女说，“给客人找几件衣服来换一换吧。顺便，我也要换一换。只是我先得去洗个澡，因为我大概打春天起就没洗过澡了。两位先生，你们愿意到浴棚里去吗？也好让他们趁这工夫把这儿收拾一下。”

美丽的佩拉格娅那么殷勤，看上去又那么温柔，她给他们送来了毛巾和肥皂，阿廖欣就陪着客人到浴棚里去了。

“是啊，我已经很久没有洗澡了，”他一面脱衣服一面说，“你们看，我的浴棚挺好，这还是我父亲盖起来的，可是不知怎的，我总是没工夫洗澡。”

他在台阶上坐下，给他的长头发和脖子擦满肥皂，他四周的水就变成棕色了。

“是啊，我看也是……”伊万·伊万内奇瞧着他的头，

意味深长地说。

“我已经很久没洗过澡了……”阿廖欣难为情地重说一遍，又用肥皂洗起来，他四周的水就变成深蓝色，跟墨水一样了。

伊万·伊万内奇走到外面去，扑通一声跳进水里，冒着雨抡开了胳膊游泳。他把身旁的水搅起波浪，睡莲就在水波上摇晃。他游到河中央水深处，扎一个猛子，过一分钟又在另一个地方钻出来，再往远处游去，老是扎猛子，极力想够到河底。“哎呀，我的上帝啊！……”他反复说着，游得痛快极了。“哎呀，我的上帝啊！……”他游到磨坊那儿，跟几个农民谈了一阵，再游回来，到了河中央就平躺在水面上，让他的脸淋着雨。布尔金和阿廖欣已经穿好衣服，准备走了，可是他还在游泳，扎猛子。

“哎呀，我的上帝啊！……”他说，“哎呀，求主怜恤我！……”

“您也游得够了！”布尔金对他喊道。

他们回到房子里。等到楼上的大客厅里点上灯，布尔金和伊万·伊万内奇都穿上了丝绸长袍和暖和的便鞋，在圈椅上坐下。阿廖欣本人也洗好脸，梳好头，穿好新

上衣，在客厅里走来走去，显然因为换了干衣服、轻便的鞋子，身上温暖洁净而感到满足。一直等到俊俏的佩拉格娅不出声地在地毯上走着，温柔地微笑，用盘子端来加了果酱的茶，一直到了这时候，伊万·伊万内奇才开口讲他的故事，而且仿佛不光是布尔金和阿廖欣在听，就连藏在金边镜框里、严厉而沉静地瞧着他们的那些老老少少的太太以及军官也在听似的。

“我们一共弟兄两个，”他开口了，“我伊万·伊万内奇和弟弟尼古拉·伊万内奇，他比我小两岁。我学技术做了兽医。尼古拉从十九岁起就已经在税务局里工作了。家父奇姆沙－吉马莱斯基本来是个世袭兵[1]，不过后来当上了军官，给我们留下世袭的贵族身份和一份小小的田产。他死后，那份小田产抵了债，可是，不管怎样，我们的童年是在乡间自由自在地度过的。我们完全跟农民的孩子一样，一天到晚在田野上，在树林里度过，看守马匹，剥树皮，钓鱼，等等。……你们要知道，谁一生当中哪怕只钓到过一次鲈鱼，或者在秋天只见过一次鸫鸟南飞，看它们怎样在晴朗凉爽的日子里成群飞过村庄，

1. 在 19 世纪中叶的俄国，兵士的儿子从出生的那天起就编入军籍，到相当年龄就入军事学校受训。

那他就再也不想做城里人了，他一直到死都会向往那种自由的生活。我弟弟在税务局里老是惦记乡下。一年年过去了，他一直坐在他那老位子上，老是抄写那些文件，老是想着一件事：怎样才能回到乡下去。他的这种苦恼渐渐成为明确的渴望，化成梦想，只求找个靠河或者近湖的地方给自己买下一个小小的庄园才好。”

“他是个温和善良的人，我喜欢他，可是这种把自己关在自家小庄园里过一辈子的愿望，我却素来不同情。人们通常说：一个人只需要三俄尺的土地[1]。可是要知道，需要三俄尺土地的是死尸，而不是活人。现在还有人说，要是我们的知识分子向往土地，盼望有个庄园，那是好事。可是要知道，这些庄园跟三俄尺土地差不多。离开城市，离开斗争，离开生活的喧嚣，隐居起来，躲在自己的庄园里，这算不得生活，这是自私自利，偷懒，这也算是一种修道主义，可又是不见成绩的修道主义。人所需要的不是三俄尺土地，也不是一个庄园，而是整个地球，整个大自然，在那广阔的天地中人才能够尽情发挥他自由精神的所有品质和特点。

“我的弟弟尼古拉坐在他的办公室里，梦想将来怎样

1.1 俄尺等于 0.711 米，3 俄尺的土地指墓穴的长度。

喝他自己家里的白菜汤，那种令人馋涎欲滴的香气弥漫在整个院子里。怎样在绿草地上吃饭，怎样在太阳底下睡觉，一连好几个钟头坐在大门外的凳子上眺望田野和树林。农艺书和日历上一切有关农艺方面的意见给了他乐趣，成了他心爱的精神食粮。他还喜欢看报，可是他光看报纸上的一种广告，说某地有若干俄亩[1]田地，连同草场、庄园、小溪、花园、磨坊和活水的池塘等一并出售。他脑子里就暗暗描出花园的幽径、花卉、水果、椋鸟巢、池塘里的鲫鱼，总之，你们知道，诸如此类的东西。这些想象的图画因他看到的广告不同而有所不同，可是不知什么缘故，其中每一个画面都一定有醋栗。他不能想象一个庄园，一个饶有诗意的安乐窝里会没有醋栗。

"'乡村生活自有它舒服的地方，'他常说，'人可以在露台上坐着，喝喝茶，自己养的小鸭子在池塘里泅水，空中弥漫着好闻的气味，而且……而且醋栗成熟了。'

"他常描画他田庄的草图，而每一回他的草图上都离不了这几样东西：(一)主人的正房，(二)仆人的下房，(三)菜园，(四)醋栗。他生活节俭，省吃省喝，上帝才知道他穿的是什么衣服，活像个叫花子；他不断地攒钱，存

1.1 俄亩等于 1.09 公顷。

在银行里。他成了财迷。我一瞧见他就痛心，常给他点钱，遇到过节也总要寄点钱给他，可是他连这点钱也收藏起来。一个人要是打定了主意，那你就拿他没办法了。

“若干年过去了，他调到另一个省里去了。他年纪已经过了四十岁，却仍旧看报上的广告，存钱。后来我听说他结婚了。他仍旧存心要买一个有醋栗的庄园，娶一个年老而难看的寡妇，对她一点感情也谈不上，只是因为她有几个钱罢了。跟她结婚以后，他生活仍旧吝啬，老是弄得她吃不饱，同时，把她的钱存在银行里，却写上他自己的名字。早先她嫁给一个邮政局长，跟他一块儿过活的时候，吃惯馅饼，喝惯果子露酒，可是跟第二个丈夫一块儿过日子，却连黑面包也吃不饱。过着这样的生活，她开始憔悴，不出三年就把灵魂交给上帝了[1]。当然，我的弟弟根本也没想过她的死要由他负责。金钱跟白酒一样，会把人变成怪物。从前我们城里有个垂危的商人。他临死叫人给他端来一碟蜂蜜，把他所有的钱钞和彩票就着蜜一股脑儿吃到肚子里，叫谁也得不着。有一回我正在一个火车站检查畜群，正巧有个马贩子失足摔在火车头底下，压断了一条腿。我们把他抬到急诊

1. 意思是“死了”。

室里，血哗哗地流，样子真是可怕，可是他老是求大家找回他的腿，老是放心不下：原来那条压断的腿所穿的靴子里有二十卢布，他生怕那点钱丢了。”

“您岔到别的事情上去了。”布尔金说。

“我的弟媳死后，”伊万·伊万内奇沉吟了半分钟，接着说，“我弟弟就开始给他自己物色一份田产。当然，尽管物色了五年，到头来仍旧会出错，买下来的东西跟所想望的迥然不同。我弟弟尼古拉托中人买了一个抵押过的庄园，有一百一十二俄亩，有主人的正房，有仆人的下房，有花园，可是单单没有果树园，没有醋栗，没有池塘和小鸭子。河倒是有，可是河水的颜色跟咖啡一样，因为庄园的一边是造砖厂，另一边是烧兽骨的工场[1]。”

“可是我的尼古拉·伊万内奇倒也并不十分难过，他订购二十株醋栗树，栽好，照地主的排场过起来了。

“去年我去探望他。我心想我要去看看那儿的情况怎么样。我弟弟在来信上称它为‘楚木巴罗克洛夫芜园，又称希马莱斯科耶’。我是在下午到达那个‘又称希马莱斯科耶’的。天很热。到处都是沟渠、围墙、篱笆、栽成一行行的杉树，弄得人不知道怎样才能走到院子里去，

1. 烧兽骨是为了制胶。

应该把马拴在哪儿。我往正房走去，迎面遇见一条红毛的肥狗，活像一头猪。它本想叫一声，可又懒得叫。厨娘从厨房里走出来，是一个光脚的胖女人，看样子也像一头猪。她说主人吃过饭后正在休息。我走进去看我弟弟。他在床上坐着，膝上盖着一条被子。他老了，胖了，皮肉发松，他的脸颊、鼻子、嘴唇，全都往前拱出去，眼看就要跟猪那样呼噜呼噜叫着钻进被子里去了。

“我们互相拥抱，流下了眼泪，一半因为高兴，一半也因为忧郁地想到，从前我们都年轻，现在两人却白发苍苍，快要入土了。他穿好衣服，领我出去看他的田庄。

“‘哦，您在这儿过得怎么样？’我问。

“‘哦，还不坏，感谢上帝，我过得挺好。’

“他不再是往日那个畏畏缩缩的、可怜的小职员，而是真正的地主老爷了。他已经在这儿住熟，习惯，觉得很有味道了。他吃得很多，常到澡棚去洗澡，长得胖起来，已经跟村社和两个工厂打过官司，遇上农民不称呼他‘老爷’，就老大地不高兴。他还带着老爷气派郑重其事地关心他的灵魂的得救，就做起好事来，然而并不是简简单单地做，却是摆足了架子做的。然而那是什么样的好事啊！他用苏打和蓖麻子油给农民治各种病，到了他的命

名日就在村子中央做一回谢恩祈祷，然后摆出半桶白酒来请农民喝，自以为事情就该这么办。啊，那可怕的半桶白酒！今天，这位胖地主拉着农民们到地方行政长官那儿去控告他们放出牲畜来践踏他的庄稼，明天遇上隆重的节日，却请那些农民喝半桶白酒。他们喝酒，嚷着：'乌拉！'喝醉了的人就给他叩头。生活只要变得好一点，吃得饱，喝得足，闲着不做事，就会在俄罗斯人身上培养出顶骄横的自大。尼古拉·伊万内奇当初在税务局里自己甚至不敢有自己的见解，现在说起话来却没有一句不是真理，而且总是用大臣的口气：'教育是必不可少的，然而对老百姓来说，还未免言之过早。''总的来说体罚是有害的，可是遇到某些情形，这却是有益的，不可缺少的。'

"'我了解老百姓，我会善于对付他们，'他说，'老百姓都喜欢我。我只要动一动手指头，老百姓就会把我要办的事统统给我办好。'

"请注意，这些话都是带着聪明而善良的笑容说出来的。他把'我们这些贵族''我以贵族的身份看来'反反复复说了二十遍。他分明已经不记得我们的祖父是个庄稼汉、父亲是个兵了。就连我们的姓，奇姆沙－希马

莱斯基，实际上十分古怪，可他现在也觉着响亮、高贵，十分中意了。

“可是问题不在他，而在我自己了。我要跟你们讲一讲我在他那庄园上盘桓了短短几个钟头，我自己起了什么变化。傍晚，我们正在喝茶，厨娘端来满满一盘醋栗放在桌子上。这不是买来的，而是他自己家里种的，自从那些灌木栽下以后，这还是头一回收果子。尼古拉·伊万内奇笑起来，对那些醋栗默默地瞧了一会儿，眼泪汪汪，激动得说不出话来。然后他拿起一颗果子送进嘴里，瞧着我，现出小孩子终于得到心爱的玩具那种得意的神情，说：

“‘多么好吃啊！’

“他贪婪地吃着，不住地重复道：

“‘嘿，多么好吃啊！你尝一尝吧！’

“那些醋栗又硬又酸，可是正如普希金所说：‘我们喜爱使人高兴的谎话，胜过喜爱许许多多的真理。’[1] 我看见了一个幸福的人，他心心念念的梦想显然已经实现，他的生活目标已经达到，他所想望的东西已经到手，他

1. 引自普希金的诗《英雄》，但引文不全，原文是：“我们喜爱使人高兴的谎话，胜过喜爱许许多多卑微的真理。”——俄文本编者注

对他的命运和他自己都满意了。不知什么缘故，往常我一想到人的幸福，就不免带一点哀伤的感觉，这一回亲眼看到幸福的人，我竟生出一种跟绝望相近的沉重感。夜里我心头特别沉重。他们在我弟弟卧室的隔壁房间里为我搭好一张床，我听见他没有睡着，老是爬下床来，走到那盘醋栗跟前，拿果子吃。我心想：实际上有多少满足而幸福的人啊！这是一种多么令人压抑的力量！你们来看一看这种生活吧：强者骄横而懒惰，弱者无知而且跟牲畜那样生活着，处处都是叫人难以忍受的贫穷、拥挤、退化、酗酒、伪善、撒谎……可是偏偏所有的屋子里也好，街上也好，却一味地心平气和，安安静静。一个城市的五万居民当中竟没有一个人叫喊一声，大声发泄一下他的愤慨。我们看见人们到市场上去买食物，白天吃饭，晚上睡觉，他们说废话，结婚，衰老，心平气和地送死人到墓园去。可是那些受苦受难的人，那些在幕后什么地方正在进行着的人生惨事，我们却没看见，也没听见。处处都安静而太平，提抗议的只有那些没声音的统计表：若干人发了疯，若干桶白酒喝光了，若干儿童死于营养不良……这样的世道显然是必要的，幸福的人之所以会感到逍遥自在，显然只是因为那些不幸的

人沉默地背着他们的重担，而缺了这种沉默想要幸福就办不到。这是普遍的麻木不仁。每一个幸福而满足的人的房门边都应当站上一个人，拿一个小锤子经常敲着门，提醒他：天下还有不幸的人，不管他自己怎样幸福，生活早晚会向他伸出魔爪，灾难会降临——疾病啦，贫穷啦，损失啦，到那时候谁也不会看见他，谁也不会听见他，就跟现在他看不见别人，听不见别人一样。可是却没有拿小锤子的人，幸福的人无忧无虑地生活下去，日常的小烦恼微微地扰动他，就跟风吹动白杨一样，真是天下太平。”

“那天晚上我才明白：我也幸福而满足，”伊万·伊万内奇站起来接着说，“我在吃饭和打猎的时候也教导过别人，应该怎样生活，怎样信仰宗教，怎样驾驭老百姓。我也常说学问是光明，教育是必不可少的，可是对普通人来说，目前只要认得字，能写字，也就够了。我常说：自由是好东西，我们生活中不能没有它，就跟不能没有空气一样，不过我们得等待。对了，我常说那样的话，现在我却要问：为什么要等？”伊万·伊万内奇生气地瞧着布尔金问道，“我问你们，为什么要等？根据什么理由？人家对我说，什么事都不是一下子就能办到的，各

种思想都要渐渐地到一定的时期才能在生活里实现。可是这话是谁说的？有什么证据能够证明这话对？你们引证事物的自然规律，引证社会现象的合法性，可是我，一个有思想的活人，站在一道壕沟面前，本来也许可以从上面跳过去，或者在上面搭座桥走过去，却偏要等它自动封口，或者等它让淤泥填满，难道这样的事还说得上什么规律和合法性？再说一遍，为什么要等？等到没有了生活的力量才算吗？可是人又非生活不可，而且也渴望生活！”

“我一清早就离开了我弟弟的家，从此我在城里住着就感到不能忍受。城里的那种和平安静压得我不好受。我不敢看人家的窗子，因为这时候再也没有比幸福的一家人团团围住桌子喝茶的光景更使我难受的了。我已经老了，不适宜做斗争了，我甚至不会憎恨人了。我只能满心地悲伤，生气，烦恼，一到夜里，我的脑子里种种思想纷至沓来，弄得我十分激动，睡不着觉……唉，要是我年轻点就好了！”

伊万·伊万内奇激动得从这个墙角走到那个墙角，反复地说：

“要是我年轻就好了！”

他忽然走到阿廖欣面前，先是握住他的一只手，后来又握住他的另一只手。

“帕维尔·康斯坦丁内奇！”他用恳求的声调说，“不要心平气和，不要容您自己昏睡！趁您还年轻力壮，血气方刚，要永不疲倦地做好事情！幸福是没有的，也不应当有。如果生活有意义，有目标，那意义和目标就绝不是我们自己的幸福，而是比这更伟大更合理的东西。做好事吧！”

所有这些话，伊万·伊万内奇都是带着可怜的、恳求的笑脸说出来的，仿佛他本人为自己请求一桩什么事似的。

然后这三个人在客厅里挑了三张圈椅各据一方坐下来，沉默了。伊万·伊万内奇的故事既没满足布尔金，也没满足阿廖欣。金边镜框里的将军们和太太们在昏光中显得像是活人，低下眼睛来瞧他们，在这样的时候听那个可怜的、吃醋栗的文官的故事觉得乏味得很。不知什么缘故他们很想谈一谈或者听一听高雅的人和女人的事。他们所在的这个客厅里，样样东西，蒙着套子的枝形烛架啦，圈椅啦，脚底下的地毯啦，都在述说如今在镜框里低下眼睛瞧他们的那些人，从前就在这房间里走

动过，坐过，喝过茶，现在俊俏的佩拉格娅正在这儿没一点声音地走来走去，这倒比一切故事都美妙得多呢。

阿廖欣困得要命，他一清早两点多钟就起床干农活儿，现在他的眼皮粘在一起了，可是他生怕客人等他走后也许会讲出什么有趣的故事，就流连着没走。他并没细想伊万·伊万内奇刚才所讲的是不是有道理、正确，反正他的客人没谈起麦粒，也没谈起干草，也没谈起煤焦油，所谈的都是跟他的生活没有什么直接关系的事，他不由得暗自高兴，盼望他们接着谈下去才好……

“不过，现在该睡了，”布尔金说，站起来，“请允许我跟你们道一声晚安吧。”

阿廖欣道了晚安，走下楼回到自己的住处去。客人们仍旧待在楼上。他俩被人领到一个大房间里过夜，房间里安着两张旧的雕花木床，墙角有一个象牙的耶稣受难像的十字架。那两张凉快的大床由美丽的佩拉格娅铺好了被褥，新洗过的床单冒出好闻的气味。

伊万·伊万内奇一声不响地脱掉衣服，躺下。

“主啊，饶恕我们这些罪人吧！”他说，拉过被子来蒙上头。

他的烟斗放在桌子上，冒出一股浓烈的烟草的焦气。

布尔金很久睡不着觉，不住地纳闷儿，想不出这股难闻的气味是打哪儿来的。

雨点通宵抽打着窗子。